PRAISE FOR THE DE

Here are some of the over 100,000 five star reviews left for the Dead Cold Mystery series.

"Rex Stout and Michael Connelly have spawned a protege."

AMAZON REVIEW

"So begins one damned fine read."

AMAZON REVIEW

"Mystery that's more brain than brawn."

AMAZON REVIEW

"I read so many of this genre...and ever so often I strike gold!"

AMAZON REVIEW

"This book is filled with action, intrigue, espionage, and everything else lovers of a good thriller want."

AMAZON REVIEW

KNIFE EDGE

A DEAD COLD MYSTERY

BLAKE BANNER

RIGHTHOUSE

Copyright © 2024 by Right House

All rights reserved.

The characters and events portrayed in this ebook are fictitious. Any similarity to real persons, living or dead, is coincidental and not intended by the author.

No part of this book may be reproduced in any form or by any electronic or mechanical means, including information storage and retrieval systems, without written permission from the author, except for the use of brief quotations in a book review.

ISBN-13: 978-1-63696-312-9

ISBN-10: 1-63696-312-9

Cover design by: Damonza

Printed in the United States of America

www.righthouse.com

www.instagram.com/righthousebooks

www.facebook.com/righthousebooks

twitter.com/righthousebooks

DEAD COLD MYSTERY SERIES
An Ace and a Pair (Book 1)
Two Bare Arms (Book 2)
Garden of the Damned (Book 3)
Let Us Prey (Book 4)
The Sins of the Father (Book 5)
Strange and Sinister Path (Book 6)
The Heart to Kill (Book 7)
Unnatural Murder (Book 8)
Fire from Heaven (Book 9)
To Kill Upon A Kiss (Book 10)
Murder Most Scottish (Book 11)
The Butcher of Whitechapel (Book 12)
Little Dead Riding Hood (Book 13)
Trick or Treat (Book 14)
Blood Into Wine (Book 15)
Jack In The Box (Book 16)
The Fall Moon (Book 17)
Blood In Babylon (Book 18)
Death In Dexter (Book 19)
Mustang Sally (Book 20)
A Christmas Killing (Book 21)
Mommy's Little Killer (Book 22)
Bleed Out (Book 23)

Dead and Buried (Book 24)
In Hot Blood (Book 25)
Fallen Angels (Book 26)
Knife Edge (Book 27)
Along Came A Spider (Book 28)
Cold Blood (Book 29)
Curtain Call (Book 30)

ONE

"I wish," she said, "it was as easy as just being color-blind. But the problem isn't really that the color of our skin is different. It isn't even a question of race. It's much deeper than that. And however hard the Mitchells tried, at the end of the day, they were the mighty white intellectuals, and Leroy was a black orphan they were trying to rescue. They tried not to see it that way, but that was the way Leroy saw it."

She paused and gazed down at her Styrofoam cup on the Formica interrogation-room table. It was a sad gaze in a beautiful face. She turned the cup around several times, like she was trying to find some redeeming feature about it but knew she wouldn't. In the end it was just a white Styrofoam cup full of black coffee.

"I guess that sounds selfish and ungrateful to you, but to a lot of black people, charity and help is like the final insult." She raised large, black eyes to look at me. "White people brought us to this condition, now they want to tell us, 'You will never make it alone, you need white men to achieve anything.'" She paused again and returned her gaze to the cup. "I didn't see it that way. I don't. I was grateful, especially to Emma Mitchell. She took Leroy into her family, into her home, like he was her own child. At least, she tried real hard to make it seem that way. Though he never really believed it. Trust was hard for him."

"What made it hard for him to trust, Sonia?"

She thought about it. "I should start from the beginning."

"I'd be grateful. I am not familiar with this case."

She sighed and sagged back in her chair. She thought for a moment and said, "My sister, Cherise, she got involved with this man. I say 'man' for want of a better word. Earl Brown, he was no good"—she darted me a glance—"like so many men, I am afraid to say. He always had a bottle in his hand, beer, whiskey, whatever. And in the other hand he always had a joint. What he never had was a steady job, and if ever he got one, he made damn sure it didn't last. He was a bad man, but we didn't realize how bad he was until it was too late."

"What happened?"

"She had two children by him, Leroy and Shevron. Like I said, he was never at work. He was at home all the time, watching TV, drinking, and smoking weed. So it was *she* had to go out to work to feed the family and keep a roof over their heads." She paused to stare at the wall. "Eight years they went on like that. I told her, more times than I can remember, 'You have got to get rid of that man, Cherise! You have got to be *free* of that man!' But she never listened. Women can be just as stupid as men sometimes. She made excuses for him, justified him, and supported that evil parasite right to the end."

She paused again and took a deep breath. "One day, I remember it like it was just yesterday: May 14, 2010, she come home early from work because she didn't feel well. She was sick. She opened the door, the front door of the house, it opened right onto the living room from the street, and she sees Leroy sitting in the armchair watching his daddy rape his little sister, Shevron. She's only six years old, and that bastard was there raping her. Well, it turned out later, he'd been doing that for years, to both of the kids."

"So what did your sister do?"

"What did she do? What would you do? What would I do? What would anybody do? She dropped her bag and ran for the kitchen. She grabbed the kitchen knife and ran at him, screaming like a wild thing. They had an almighty fight."

She shook her head. Her bottom lip curled in, and tears balanced on her eyelids then spilled onto her cheek.

"It's ten years ago, maybe more, but it feels like it was just this morning. There was a big fight. A real big fight. Little Shevron tried to protect her mother, and that bastard killed her for it, hit her so hard he broke her neck. Then, it seems, Cherise stabbed Earl in the back with the kitchen knife. Should have killed him, but somehow he took it from her and stabbed her several times in the belly, in some kind of frenzy, before he collapsed and they both died."

I frowned and raised a hand to stop her. "How do you know this, Sonia?"

She nodded, as though she agreed with the question. "Leroy was so traumatized his memory was pretty vague, but he witnessed everything. Also, the medical examiner and the investigating detectives pieced it all together that way, by the position of the bodies and where the wounds were. And it all made sense. It was the only way it could have happened."

She paused, gathering her thoughts.

"Several of the neighbors called the cops when they heard the screams and shouts. I think there was a couple of them the cops were interested in for a while, but they had alibis, and in the end they figured it went down the way they said, they killed each other and left poor Leroy alone in the world."

"You didn't adopt him?"

"I couldn't. I live alone and I work long hours. There was no way I could afford the money or the time to look after a traumatized kid of eight." She shook her head, confirming the impossibility. "No, he went to the orphanage. But not for long. The Mitchells had read about the murder, they live in the Bronx, and they offered to adopt him. They changed his name. Dr. Mitchell,

Brad, said it would help him to reinvent himself after the trauma, but I believe it just sounded less black to them than Leroy."

"What can you tell me about the Mitchells?"

"They are both academics. They lecture at NYU, he is a psychiatrist, I think, and she is in sociology or women's studies or something like that. Anyhow, there was a lot of debate and discussion about whether a white family should adopt a black kid. Brad accused the orphanage of instigating apartheid through the back door and said he would sue them and have them shut down, so they agreed to approve the adoption, and Leroy went to live with them about six months after the murder."

I cleared my throat and scratched my head. "Was he seeing a therapist of any sort at that time?"

"Yes, the court appointed a child psychologist to see him on a regular basis. Ms. Simone Robles. He saw her once a week to begin with, but it was less than that, about once a month, by the time . . ."

She hesitated. She looked away, blinking.

"Let's stay with his move to the Mitchells for now. He was what, eight, nine?"

"He was still only eight."

"How did he get on with the Mitchells? They had children of their own?"

She nodded. "They were very nice to him, and at first he appreciated that. They were good, kind people, especially Emma. With Brad, even though he was a good man, you always felt he was doing what he was doing out of a sense of principle, or obligation. He believed he should be doing it, so he did it. But with Emma . . ." She smiled. "With her you felt it was more from the heart. She was warmer."

"They had kids?" I asked again.

"They had two kids, a little younger than Leroy. There was Marcus, who was about six or seven, and Lea, who was four or five."

"And how did Leroy get on with Marcus and Lea?"

She nodded several times, looking down at the Formica top of the table. Eventually she said, "They got on well. He was maybe too keen to please, too excitable, but the whole family was kind and patient and tolerant, and very slowly he began to settle down into the family. Marcus was real kind to him, called him his brother. Everything was fine, or at least it seemed to be fine."

"You mean it wasn't? Was there something you didn't know about?"

She heaved a big, heavy sigh. "I don't know. For four years he seemed to be happy, in as much as he could be. But when he turned twelve, in August 2013, his attitude started to change. He started talking a lot of stupid crap about blacks and whites, about how black men were better and stronger than white men, about how white women preferred black men—I don't know where he was getting that stuff, but it began to worry me."

"He was in touch with you, obviously."

"He used to come visit with me. Sometimes he'd stay the weekend. We used to write WhatsApp messages to each other. He loved his aunt"—she smiled—"but when I told him he was talking a lot of BS, and that God made all men and women equal, he told me I didn't know what I was talking about. That made me unhappy. I told him I did not want him talking like that in front of the Mitchells. He promised me he wouldn't, but I didn't really believe him.

"I spoke to Emma about it once, and she told me not to worry about it. She said he had had a very traumatic experience and it would take him years to deal with it and come to terms with it. What he was doing with all that racist rubbish was to try and find his own identity, his own sense of self, and for that he would have to go through a lot of garbage. She was a wonderful woman, Detective Stone."

"So what happened?"

"Just about a week after we talked, I got a phone call from Emma. She told me Leroy had been killed, and so had her little girl, Lea. Marcus had not been hurt"—she jabbed at her body with her fingertips—"physically, but he was in a bad state of shock, and he was being seen by a psychiatrist."

The story was new to me. I had vague memories of having read something about it, and hearing talk at the station house, but I had not retained any of the details. I frowned. "How were they killed?"

"It was Sunday, June 13. Brad and Emma had been sitting drinking coffee after breakfast and the kids were playing in the backyard. It was a big area." She stretched out her hands to indicate it was large. "They had a big lawn with trees at the end, and flower beds and stuff, and they had a garden shed where they kept the gardening tools and flowerpots . . ." She trailed off.

"What happened?"

"They were having coffee, like I said, and suddenly they heard a lot of screaming. Brad said it sounded hysterical. They recognized the voices of the kids, and they ran to see what was going on. According to Brad, the voices were coming from the garden shed. They rushed to see what had happened, thinking maybe one of the kids had hurt themselves with one of the tools. But it was much worse than that."

She placed her fingertips over her mouth, as though she was receiving the shock all over again. She closed her eyes and spoke in a strange monotone, like some kind of android.

"They found Lea and Leroy dead on the floor of the shed. Emma said there was blood everywhere. The floor was thick . . ." She shook her head without opening her eyes. "Thick, with blood. Lea had had her throat cut, and Leroy had been stabbed in the back, repeatedly, as if in a frenzy."

"What about . . ." I checked my notes. "Marcus? Where was Marcus?"

"They found him, poor kid, they found him hiding under a tarp in the shed. He was shivering, and the ME said he was in a deep state of shock. He couldn't speak."

"But"—my frown deepened—"they must have spoken to him eventually. What did he say had happened?"

She shook her head. "No, the doctor said he needed time to get over the shock, but he gradually slipped into a catatonic depression, which just got worse. He never spoke again—from that morning on, till now, he hasn't said a word. And as far as I know he hasn't got out of bed."

I scribbled some notes and asked, "What was the outcome of the investigation, do you know?"

"It was never solved. There was no DNA other than the kids', nor any . . ." She made little flapping motions with her hand.

I said, "Forensic evidence?"

She nodded. "Yes, forensic evidence. And the only witness, as far as they could tell, was Marcus. And he wasn't talking. So the case went cold."

I leaned back in my chair and tapped my pen on my notepad.

"As far as I can tell, from what you've told me, Sonia, there is nothing new here. You've described the two murders, very clearly and concisely"—I smiled at her—"and thank you for that, but there is nothing new. Unless we have some fresh evidence, it is hard to see how we can go any further with the investigation."

She nodded at her hands clasped on the table, but she didn't move. I watched her narrowly for a moment, then went on.

"But you didn't come here after six years just to repeat to me what I could have found in the file. Has something new come up? Is there something that wasn't mentioned in the original investigation?"

She sighed again. "Not exactly. You see . . ." She stopped, then started again. "I told you that Leroy started going through a difficult phase, where he was rebelling against Brad and Emma."

"Sure, it didn't seem to worry them too much."

"Well, what they didn't know was that he wrote me a text message one day, a couple of weeks before . . ." She faltered again.

I said, "Before the crime."

"Yes, before the crime. In that message he said that he knew Brad was seeing another woman. He'd heard him on the phone, talking quietly, and he said he'd seen messages. So he cut school a couple of times and went to the university, where he said he saw Brad with another woman." She reached in her purse and pulled out a cell. She opened her photographs and slid the phone across the table to me. "He sent me this picture."

It showed a tall, slim man in his early forties. He was wearing a tweed jacket and chinos and had a shock of prematurely white hair swept back from his face. He was smiling, talking to an attractive woman in her early thirties. By their expressions you'd guess they liked each other, but not much more than that. I gave my head a shake and looked at her.

"I'm afraid this proves nothing, Sonia. A university professor must speak to hundreds of people every week."

"I know, and that's why I never mentioned it at the time. I put it down to Leroy's feelings of rebellion and inadequacy about Brad. He said he was going to use the photograph to blackmail Brad. I got real mad and scolded him, and told him he should be ashamed of himself, and to be honest I never thought any more about it until last week."

"What happened last week?"

"A friend of mine at work pointed it out to me. It was an article in the paper. Brad Mitchell has opened a rehab clinic upstate, beyond White Plains, in the Silver Lake Preserve." She stopped again, rubbing the fingers of her right hand with her left.

I asked, "And . . . ?"

"The psychiatrist in charge of the Mitchell Clinic will be Dr. Margaret Wagner, the woman in that photograph."

I winced. It was close, but not close enough. "In itself," I said, "if they are colleagues, there is nothing odd about that. If they have been working together for five or six years, perhaps much longer, you would expect him to name her, a close, trusted colleague, over somebody else."

She was nodding. "Yeah, I know, and that's why I didn't come straight here. But I kept asking myself, what if there was something in what Leroy saw and heard? What if when Leroy saw them together, they were a lot more intimate than what comes across in that picture? What if he went to Brad Mitchell and did try to blackmail him? That was only six years ago; maybe they were already planning their clinic for celebrity drug addicts. That little black brat, he could have screwed it up for them for good."

I puffed out my cheeks and blew. She shook her head again. "I am not saying that's what happened. I am just asking, what if?"

I thought about it for a long moment.

"Okay, Sonia, send me the picture, I'll discuss it with my partner, and maybe we'll review the case and go and have a talk with Brad Mitchell and Dr. Wagner. I can't promise you anything, but we'll have a look and see if the lead is worth following."

She smiled and thanked me, and sat a moment. I figured she was in her late forties. She was attractive and elegant but looked tired, drawn, and unhappy. Finally she stood and left, and I reached for my cell.

TWO

The phone rang three times before she picked it up. When she spoke, she was out of breath.

"Yeah, Stone, what's up?"

"Where are you?"

"I'm working out in the gym, why?"

"Because we're going to visit Brad and Emma Mitchell, in Castle Hill."

"Uh-huh. Why?"

"Git yer ass up to your desk and you can read why in the file."

I heard a soft grunt. "I love when you talk rough like that, you bad, bad man."

I hung up and went down to my desk to sort through our cardboard filing system, comprised of two large cartons, and found *Brown 2010*, and *Mitchell 2014*. They were cross-referenced. I read them over briefly, called Frank, the ME, about something I didn't understand, and was making copies of the two files when Dehan walked in, looking fresh and lithe. I shoved a file in her hands.

"One," I said.

"Hello."

I ignored her and went on. "Cherise Brown, married to Earl

Brown, like so many men, a no-good, low-down drunk. She, apparently blinded by love, had two children by him, Leroy and Shevron. While he was at home watching TV, drinking whiskey, and smoking weed, she was at work raising money to feed her family. This went on for eight years. Her sister, Sonia, our informant, advised her repeatedly to leave him and start a new life, but Cherise made excuses for him, and they stayed together."

Dehan rested her ass on the side of her desk and frowned at me. I went on.

"On May 14, 2010, Cherise arrived home early from work and found Earl raping six-year-old Shevron while eight-year-old Leroy watched. It turned out later this had been going on for some years, to both of the kids."

"Son of a bitch. What did Mom do?"

"She went to the kitchen, grabbed the kitchen knife, and attacked him. There was a fight."

"In front of the kids?"

"Mm-hm, Shevron tried to protect her mother and Earl hit her so hard he broke her neck. Reconstruction by the ME and the detectives at the time was that Cherise stabbed Earl in the back, he somehow took the knife from her and stabbed her several times in the belly before collapsing, and they both died."

"Leaving Leroy as the only living witness to the violent death of his entire family. Holy sh . . ."

I nodded. "But that's not all of it."

"There's more?"

"Yup." I collected up the copies and dropped into my chair at the desk. She shifted round to look at me. "Leroy went to an orphanage for about six months. Almost immediately, as soon as the murder was reported in the press, the Mitchells, a liberal, academic family who were residents of the Bronx, applied to adopt Leroy. They both lectured at NYU. He's a psychiatrist, she a sociologist. There was some concern about whether a white family should adopt a black orphan, but after six months and threats of legal action, it was approved."

"Kid had a shrink?"

"Simone Robles. In the file. He was still only eight."

"The Mitchells had kids?"

"Two kids, younger than Leroy. Marcus, seven, and Lea, five. Apparently they got on well, and the whole family was keen to make it work. Seems the kids liked each other, but..."

"There had to be a but."

"It seems, when Leroy turned twelve, in August 2013, he began to change. He started talking to his aunt about how black men were better and stronger than white men, how white women preferred black men. He used to write her WhatsApp messages on the subject. Sonia spoke to Emma about it, but the Mitchells didn't seem too concerned. They thought it was normal given the trauma he had suffered, and he'd get over it..."

"So what happened?"

"On June 13, four years and a month, almost to the day, after his parents and his sister were killed, he was killed too, along with his adoptive sister, Lea."

"Holy cow. How were they killed?"

"It was a Sunday, Brad and Emma Mitchell had been drinking coffee after breakfast and the kids were playing in the backyard. They had a big lawn and a garden shed where they kept the gardening tools. At some point, the Mitchells started to hear a lot of screaming coming from the shed. They ran to see what it was about and found Lea and Leroy dead. There was a lot of blood on the floor. Lea had had her throat cut, and Leroy had been stabbed repeatedly in the back."

Dehan was frowning hard. "What about the other boy, Marcus?"

"They found him in the shed, hiding under a tarpaulin. He was in severe shock. He hasn't been able to help as a witness because he slipped into a catatonic depression and never really recovered. He has never spoken again, to this day."

"Huh!"

"It was never solved. There was no DNA or forensic evidence, and the case went cold."

She nodded. "And the only witness was the kid, Marcus."

"Yup."

"Okay . . ." She moved around to her chair and sat in it. "But I don't see how we can do anything with this, Stone. Where the hell do you begin?"

I leaned forward with my elbows on the desk. "Sonia came to see me this morning, and she brought not so much new evidence as old evidence with a new angle. It's thin, but . . ." I shrugged. "I think it's worth a look. It seems, a couple of weeks before he was killed, Leroy—or Lee, as his new family called him—sent a WhatsApp message to his aunt telling her that he thought Brad Mitchell was having an affair. He'd heard him on the phone and, apparently, he'd seen text messages. So he'd cut school a couple of times and been to the university, where he'd seen Brad with that woman." I slid my cell across the table to her. "He sent her this picture."

She glanced at it. "So what? Proves nothing. It's not even suggestive."

"Yeah, agreed. But Sonia and a workmate found an article in the paper which said that Brad Mitchell had opened a rehab clinic near White Plains, in the Silver Lake Preserve. The psychiatrist in charge of the Mitchell Clinic was to be Dr. Margaret Wagner, the woman in that photograph."

She sagged back in her chair, made a wincing face, and blew. "You're right. It's thin. It's not thin, it's anorexic supermodel skinny."

"Yeah, I know, but Sonia makes the point, and I agree, Leroy threatened to blackmail Brad Mitchell. If the clinic was already on the cards back then, that's a pretty strong motive for murder. Especially if the victim is not your own kid, but an increasingly obnoxious intruder."

She screwed skepticism into her face. "But he'd also have to have killed his own daughter. And his wife says they were having coffee together. She's not likely to alibi him if he's killed her daughter."

I shrugged. "Yeah, but like Sonia said, what if? I think it's worth asking a few questions and finding out exactly what kind of relationship he and Dr. Wagner have."

She turned a pencil around in her fingers for a while, then said, "Yeah, I guess. So where do we start, with Dr. Wagner?"

"Yes, chances are she knows nothing about the kid's death. But all we want from her is whether she was having an affair with Mitchell. If we catch her off guard she might just come clean. If we go to Mitchell first, he'll alert her, and she could clam up."

She nodded and made to stand. "So all we are doing right now is establishing whether she and Brad Mitchell were having an affair."

"Correct."

"And then we take it from there?"

"Yup."

"Okay."

She flicked through her phone book and after a moment made a call. She sat staring at me for a moment with the phone to her ear, biting her lip. Then:

"Yeah, good morning, this is Detective Carmen Dehan of the NYPD. We would like to meet with the director of the clinic... Dr. Margaret Wagner? Okay, thanks." She winked at me and mouthed *putting me through to her secretary.* "Yeah, good afternoon. Detective Carmen Dehan of the New York Police Department. We would like to meet with the director of the clinic... Dr. Margaret Wagner? Let me just make a note... Sooner the better. Sure, today, say in about three-quarters of an hour...? Okay, that's great." Another pause, and Dehan pursed her lips and shook her head. "Oh, it's just a routine inquiry. Thanks."

She hung up and smiled. "See, Stone, I'm smart. Now her secretary thinks we had no idea the director was Dr. Wagner, and that our inquiry is about one of her patients. No red flags, no calls to Brad Mitchell."

"You are subtle, Dehan. A subtle, devious, dangerous woman. Let's go."

We stepped out into the cold midmorning light. The sun was low in the south and casting long shadows across Fteley and Story Avenues. We climbed into my ancient burgundy Jaguar Mark II and took the Bronx River Parkway north through endless green suburbs as far as Elmsford, and then turned east into White Plains. It was a half-hour drive, and by the time we got there it was eleven a.m., and the sun was approaching its zenith in a perfect blue sky. We skirted the north of the town and took Hall Avenue into deep woodland. The Brad Mitchell clinic was about a mile in on the right-hand side behind large iron gates set in a fifteen-foot, redbrick wall.

The clinic was an old Georgian manor at the end of a hundred-yard blacktop drive surrounded by sweeping lawns and woodlands. Dehan pushed her shades up onto her head and scrutinized the parkland around us.

"He's not short of a few bucks, Stone. This is a few million in real estate."

I nodded. "Two gets you twenty he has investors, which is further reason to avoid bad publicity."

We pulled up in the parking lot at the front of the building and climbed the flight of six broad granite steps to the main doors. Inside there was the kind of hush you only get with high ceilings and marble floors, where even the echoes seem distant. There was a small, discreet reception desk on the left as we went in. The girl sitting behind it smiled at us with polite indifference and asked Dehan how she could help her.

"We're here to see Dr. Wagner." Dehan showed her her badge, and I showed her mine. "Detectives Carmen Dehan and John Stone."

She picked up a phone on her solid oak desk and after a second said, "Detectives Dehan and Stone to see Dr. Wagner... mm-hm." She hung up and pointed to a broad, marble staircase that rose along the back wall of the entrance hall. "Next floor, turn right at the top of the stairs, and Dr. Wagner's office is at the end on the right."

Dehan smiled at her with dead eyes. "If I was a celebrity with a habit, would you take me there yourself?"

The receptionist didn't lose her smile or her composure. She tilted her head on one side and said, "No, Dr. Wagner would come down to meet you."

"That's what I thought."

We turned and climbed the stairs and followed her directions to the end of a long corridor carpeted in red, with prints on the walls depicting English hunt scenes and ships in full sail on the high seas. The door there was open, and through it we found an office paneled in wood, with a desk and a couple of filing cabinets. Behind the desk was a woman in her fifties with gunmetal hair and pale blue eyes that could kill a warm feeling at three hundred paces without blinking. She didn't say hello; she said, "May I see your identification, please?"

We showed her our badges, which she inspected briefly before adding, "Dr. Wagner can spare you ten minutes. Please keep the interview as brief as possible."

Neither of us answered, so she stood, moved to the door that was behind her desk and to the right, knocked, and leaned in.

"The detectives from New York, Dr. Wagner . . ."

She paused a moment, listening, then stood back and held the door open for us. As we filed past, she repeated, under her breath, "Please, keep it brief."

Dehan scowled at her. "Go file something, sister."

Dr. Wagner was standing behind her desk. Your first impression when you looked at her was that you were looking at a very attractive woman. She was tall, and elegant in her movements. She had an abundance of well-cut blond hair, deep, warm brown eyes, and skin that looked naturally youthful. Then you noticed that there were things that were wrong. She was just a bit too tall, her body was boney and angular, and her mouth was too wide. Then you looked again and realized it didn't matter, because in her it all came together and worked. I decided she was a woman a lot of men would find it easy to have an affair with.

I heard the door close behind me and moved across the room. I showed her my badge.

"Dr. Wagner, I am Detective John Stone from the New York Police Department, and this is my partner, Detective Carmen Dehan."

She smiled at Dehan and said, "Congratulations. Female detectives are still a minority. How can I help you? Please, sit down."

This last was also addressed to Dehan. The three of us sat, and I waited for Dehan to speak. Wagner spoke first.

"If it's one of our patients you are interested in, I'm afraid I *will* need a court order. We don't want to be obstructive, and we will give the broadest interpretation to any court order you have, but our patients pay a great deal for our therapies..."

Dehan was shaking her head. "We are not here about any of your patients, Dr. Wagner. We are actually here about your relationship with Dr. Brad Mitchell."

She froze. Her eyebrows rose suddenly, and her pale cheeks flushed pink.

"My..." She leaned forward slightly. "My *what*?"

Neither of us answered her. We just watched her, trying to read the signs. She laughed and shook her head. "My *relationship* with Dr. Mitchell is purely professional."

Dehan asked, "How long have you known each other?"

"I don't know!" She gazed up and to the left, shaking her head. "Ten, eleven years? Perhaps a little more. Do you mind telling me what this is about?"

Dehan shook her head. "Not at all. How did you meet? Was it at the university?"

She frowned. "Yes. We were in the same department. We were colleagues."

Dehan spread her hands, cocked her head on one side. "A little more than colleagues."

"What do you mean? No, absolutely not! We were colleagues!"

Dehan gestured at the desk with both hands. "He appointed you as the director of his clinic. That is more than just colleagues."

Now she was frowning hard, and her cheeks had deepened to red.

"I don't know what you're driving at, Detective, but there was absolutely no impropriety in my appointment to this position. I worked damn hard for it, and I earned it!"

"I have no doubt about that, Dr. Wagner. I just wanted to make the point that your relationship was not one of mere colleagues. Now that's right, isn't it, Doctor? You were not merely colleagues, were you?"

Dr. Wagner took a deep breath and let it out slow.

"All right, Detective, we were not merely colleagues. We were, and are, also good friends. We tend to play down our friendship because people do love to gossip and spread rumors. But obviously, we planned the clinic from scratch together, and eventually he put up the money, and I run the place. We are not quite partners, but that is on the cards. It is impossible to make that kind of commitment together without becoming close friends . . ."

Dehan was nodding. When Dr. Wagner trailed off, Dehan spoke patiently, almost kindly. "I had got about that far by myself, Doctor. What I am asking you is how close that friendship is."

She hesitated, looked at her desk for a while and then into Dehan's eyes. There was defiance there. "And I am going to ask you again, Detective, what is this about?"

Dehan was about to answer, but I cut in.

"It's about your affair with Dr. Mitchell. We need to know when it started, Dr. Wagner."

Her eyes went wide, and her jaw sagged slightly. Her voice, when she answered, was slightly shrill.

"I don't know where to begin! I mean . . . Quite aside from the fact that I am *not* having an affair with Brad, I *resent* your nosing around in my personal affairs! And *since when* is it the business of the police whether consenting adults have affairs or not?"

I didn't pause or hesitate. "Since those affairs might provide the motive for murder, Dr. Wagner."

"... *Murder?*"

"Yes. This is a murder inquiry, Dr. Wagner. Now, would you please answer the question? When did your affair with Dr. Mitchell begin?"

THREE

She sat for a long moment, staring at nothing a couple of inches above her desk. Eventually she frowned at her own thoughts and turned her gaze to me.

"Am I a suspect? I have a right to know. And what about Brad? Is he a suspect?"

Dehan glanced at me. Her face said my play hadn't worked out. I disagreed but shook my head at Dr. Wagner.

"You're not a suspect, Dr. Wagner. Right now we have no real suspects. What we are trying to do is establish the background against which the crime was committed." I offered her a smile which was not unkind and added, "You have already admitted with your silence that you did have an affair with Dr. Mitchell. If you hadn't, you'd have had no problem telling us so, very firmly, I would imagine. What we need to know is when it started and, if it finished, when?"

She was not happy. "If I am not a suspect, I am not under arrest . . ."

I knew where she was going, and so did Dehan. She beat me to the punch and cut her off.

"June 2014, were you together?"

Her face clamped up, but her eyes spoke volumes. Then her mouth joined in. "I think I'd like you to leave now."

I nodded once, looking out of her window at the cold, green landscape, silent and still through triple glazing. "Sure," I said, and shifted my gaze to meet her eyes. "But please bear in mind, Dr. Wagner, that if we decide you are a material witness, or even a suspect, we can have you picked up and taken into custody with a whole fleet of patrol cars, all with flashing lights and wailing sirens. If you were not involved in the murder, but you have relevant information, it is always in your interest to cooperate with us."

Her voice was almost a whisper. "What murder?"

"Were you lovers in June 2014?"

She didn't answer. I stood and took a card from my wallet and handed it to her. "Call me or Detective Dehan at these numbers, anytime, day or night. If we're not at the precinct, they'll forward the call."

Dehan pulled the door open. She paused as I went through it and turned back toward Dr. Wagner. "The victims were children, Doctor. Think about it."

We made our way down the marble stairs among cold echoes and crossed the gloomy hall, out into the bright, crisp noonday sun. In the car, we cut through White Plains and took Bloomingdale Road south until it became Mamaroneck Avenue. We followed that till we came to Lombardo's on the left. There I did a U-turn and pulled into the large parking lot.

"Pizza and lamb chops," I said to Dehan, "and cold beer."

She shook her head. "No, oysters, pizza, lamb chops, and cold beer."

"You're right." I nodded, and we climbed out of the ancient growler.

We found a booth and gave our order. Dehan drummed her fingers on the table and drew breath. I said, "It's too soon to start formulating theories, Dehan."

"I say to you what Nero Wolfe would say to you."

"And what would that be?"

"Phooey!"

I laughed. "Fine, let's hear it. And then you can tell me what it's based on."

The beers arrived, and she took a pull, then wiped the foam from her mouth with the back of her hand.

"You told Wagner she had pretty much confessed to having an affair with Mitchell when she refused to answer . . ."

"That was a bluff, Dehan, and has no probative value at all . . ."

"Shut up and listen, Stone. Sure, it has no probative value in court, but we're not in court. It's just you and me, nosing around. We both know if she hadn't been having an affair, she would have told us so right away." She made a scandalized face. "What, *me*? And *Brad*? Are you out of your *minds*?"

I smiled. "Fine. I'll shut up."

"Well, the same applies to the date. When we asked her if they were involved in June 2014, if they hadn't been she would have taken that way out and told us no way."

"Why?"

"Because clearly the date tied their affair to the murder in some way, might even make one of them a suspect. If the date had been wrong, she would have seized on that with both hands. Instead, she freaked out. She clammed up and told us to leave. That means one thing and one thing only, Stone. She was with him at that time."

"Maybe."

"Phooey, sir!"

"I think I preferred it when you read Mickey Spillane."

"They had an affair, and they were involved in June 2014, when those kids were killed. That's what we came here to find out, and that's what we found out. Now I am going to ask you the kind of question you ask: What was it about their being involved at that time that made us want to know?"

"I think I might have phrased it more tersely, with more brevity."

"Whatever. So what was it about their having an affair at that time that was important to us? Answer: if they were having an affair at that time, it increased the possibility that Brad might have reacted to Leroy's blackmail by killing him. Am I wrong?"

"No."

"So?"

"So we continue with the investigation, for now, but I am still finding it very hard to believe that Mitchell would kill his own daughter. Maybe when we meet him I'll change my mind. But right now it does not fit his profile at all. A liberal academic who adopts an orphan because he reads about him in the papers and feels compassion for him is not the obvious choice for killing his five-year-old daughter to cover up the murder of that same adopted orphan." She grunted, and I went on. "Besides, Sunday midmorning, with all the family there, is not the ideal time. Surely he could have chosen a better opportunity."

She grunted again. A moment later the waitress arrived with the oysters. She left, and we sat in relative silence, making only those noises you make when you're eating oysters. When Dehan had devoured the last of those edible, bivalve mollusks, and I had drawn off two-thirds of my beer, I smacked my lips and said, "There is something else."

She picked up a paper napkin and wiped her mouth. "What?"

"Lea, Mitchell's daughter, was killed with a knife."

"Uh-huh."

"So was Leroy."

"Okay . . ."

"And so were Leroy's mother and father."

She frowned hard at me. "You are reaching, Stone."

I screwed up my napkin and dropped it by my plate. "In 2019, six thousand, three hundred and sixty-eight people were murdered in the United States using handguns. Only one thousand, four hundred and seventy-six were murdered using knives.

That one small boy should be involved in four murders, each one a stabbing, is a statistical aberration, and therefore significant. It means something."

"It's a fluke, Stone. The first was a domestic incident, and the choice of a kitchen knife was opportunistic. It was what was available. And in the murder of Lea and Leroy . . ." She shrugged and watched the waitress take away the empty plates and deliver the pizza and a dish of lamb chops. When she'd gone, Dehan said, "Either the murders were committed by Mitchell or they weren't. If he did, we have to assume that he was under an intolerable amount of pressure caused by the threat of blackmail from Leroy that was going to bring down not only his family, but also his career and the clinic he was planning to establish. Now, think about it, Stone. What are the chances of a New York liberal academic having a gun in his house—or anywhere else for that matter?"

"Granted."

"You want to hear what my gut is saying?"

"Aside from 'feed me more pizza'?"

She stuffed a slice in her mouth and spoke around it.

"I think the killing of Leroy and Lea was also opportunistic. We don't know what went down that day. We only know what the Mitchells told the investigating detectives. But my gut tells me that *if* Mitchell killed those kids, it was a spur-of-the-moment decision in which he seized an opportunity and struck."

I shrugged. "It's very possible. But it's only speculation."

She stared at me a moment, chewing, then said, "Wagner will have telephoned Mitchell by now, and he'll be expecting us. We need to go see him while he is still rattled, before he has time to agree on a story with her."

I picked up a lamb chop and nodded. "That kind of thing takes a lot of time and thought and discussion. There is always something you overlook or forget about. We'll go see him after lunch."

She wiped her fingers on her jeans and reached for her cell.

"I'll call him now and tell him we're on our way, rattle him a little more."

She held the cell to her ear for a moment, sucking her teeth and staring at me. Then:

"Yeah, this is Detective Carmen Dehan of the NYPD, I need to talk to Dr. Brad Mitchell." She waited a moment, watching me. "Putting me through to his secretary." I nodded once, upward. She averted her eyes and started talking. "Yeah, good afternoon. This is Detective Carmen Dehan of the NYPD. I need to speak with Dr. Brad Mitchell . . . Oh, he's teaching a seminar right now? How long will he be?" She grinned at me and winked. "You figure he'll be another hour? So he's been in there for an hour already . . . Okay, well that's fine. Please let him know that we'll be there in an hour"—she looked at her watch—"at one thirty, and we really need to talk to him. It's important."

She hung up. We finished the chops and the pizza, drained our beers, and left.

An hour later I found a parking space outside the Psychology Building of New York University at Number Six, Washington Place. It was right next to the Center for Neural Science at Number Four. The two departments were in the same classic Gotham City style, with black facades at street level that somehow managed to suggest the deep unconscious, between massive, ochre columns in a neo-Greco-Roman style that added to the awe factor.

We found Mitchell's office on the ninth floor. He had the corner overlooking Washington Place and Mercer Street. It was large and classical in style, with a lot of mahogany and tall oak bookcases with well-thumbed hardbacks and paperbacks overflowing the shelves. The floor was dark green wall-to-wall carpet, and his desk and chair were oak and green leather.

Mitchell was tall and rangy, slim, with thick silver hair. He was standing beside his desk, in a dark blue suit, looking at us fixedly with his cell to his ear. He said, "Okay, they're here. I'll get back to you."

He hung up, laid his cell on the desk, and spoke as he removed his jacket and hung it on the back of his chair, like he was preparing for a fight.

"So, this is the new, human face of the New York Police Department. First you mount an incompetent investigation into my children's death, then you neglect it for six years, and finally, lacking any other suspects, you try to pin it on the father. That's good, you know?" He pulled out the chair and lowered himself into it. "Because I haven't been through enough in the last six years. I need to suffer a bit more." He paused, scowled at us, and asked, "What the hell do you want?"

I approached and showed him my badge. "Detective John Stone, of the New York Police Department. This is my partner, Detective Dehan. Dr. Mitchell, do you mind if we sit down for ten minutes? We'll make this as brief as is possible."

He sighed and gestured at the two chairs across his desk. We sat, and Dehan spoke first.

"Was that Dr. Wagner on the phone, Dr. Mitchell?"

He focused his scowl on her. "You know damn well it was. That's why you went to see her first, in the hopes of scaring me and unsettling me."

He loosened his tie.

I said, "Dr. Mitchell, I head up a cold-case unit at the Forty-Third Precinct. The first investigation ground to a halt through a total lack of evidence. But we have received new evidence, and we are bound to look into it."

His face flushed, and there was real anger in his eyes. "New evidence? Just what exactly do you call evidence in the New York Police Department? Rumors? Malicious gossip?"

I offered him a rueful smile. "Anything we can get our hands on, sir. It's possible we are clutching at straws, Dr. Mitchell. But in investigating the murder of two children, I would rather clutch at straws than ignore a possible lead so as not to offend somebody."

He closed his eyes and took a deep breath. After a moment he opened them again.

"I am not having an affair with Dr. Wagner, and I have never had an affair with Dr. Wagner. Does that answer your question? And please, before you go *blundering* about in your so-called investigation, bear in mind the enormous damage you could do to my career, Dr. Wagner's career, and my family. I *think*, Detectives, that we have been through enough in recent years, without this ham-fisted attempt to pin my daughter's murder on me."

Dehan raised an eyebrow. "What about Leroy?"

He frowned at her for a moment like he didn't understand what she was saying. "You mean Lee. You can't be so naïve as to think that Lee's death devastated me as much as my daughter's. I have been a psychiatrist for thirty years, and I have been in analysis for every one of those years. I am not going to sit here and lie about the most central, important things in my life. I was learning to love Lee. I certainly cared about him and his welfare. But we all knew, from the very start, that it was not going to be easy. He was a troubled and conflicted boy, and in the last year he was with us he made it *hard* to like him. Even so, Emma and I stayed the course and supported each other, and we were learning to love him."

He shook his head, and tears welled in his eyes. "But Lea . . . Not a day goes by that my heart does not break when I remember her. I long for her and weep for her. I didn't need to learn to love her. I loved her from before she was born. It's neurology, hormones, brain chemistry, whatever you like. That's how human beings work. It doesn't change the fact that she was my baby girl, I love her still, and I will love her to the day I die."

It looked sincere, but after thirty years studying the human mind and how emotions work, I was prepared to hedge my bets.

"Were you aware, Dr. Mitchell, that Lee had told his aunt, Sonia, that he believed you were having an affair with Dr. Wagner, that he had followed you to the university and taken photographs of you?"

"Yes." He gave a single nod. "I was aware of that."

"Were you aware that it was his intention to blackmail you with that information?"

"He told me that, yes. He came to my den in the house, knocked on my door, and came in. He showed me the photographs he had and told me he wanted a hundred bucks a week to keep silent about it. Otherwise he would tell my wife."

The room was very quiet for a moment. Then Dehan asked, "Do you not agree, Dr. Mitchell, that what he did provided you with a very powerful motive for murder?"

His face was like granite. He held her eye for a long moment, then said, "Yes, I do. I'd say it provides a very powerful motive for murder indeed."

FOUR

"I'll tell you." He laid both of his large hands on the edge of his desk and examined them. "I'll tell you what I did. He sat there, across from me, with an impudent sneer on his face, and what I wanted to do was what my father would have done to me, if I had dared speak to him the way Lee spoke to me. What I wanted to do was lay him across my knee and beat him soundly with my slipper."

He paused, and there was still anger in his eyes. "But what I did, what I *did*, Detectives, was to laugh in his face and call my wife. When she arrived, I showed her the photographs and told her what Lee had said. She laughed too, and we tried to have a dialogue with him, to make him understand that he did not need to blackmail love out of us. We were ready to love him anyway. He ran out of my study in a tantrum and slammed his way up the stairs and into his room."

"Will your wife corroborate that?"

He picked up his phone and dialed, then held it out to me across his desk. "Ask her yourself."

I heard it ring a couple of times and then a cultured, female voice came on the line. It spoke with warmth.

"Hello, darling. What are you doing calling me at this time?"

"Dr. Mitchell, this is not your husband. He has given me his phone to speak to you."

"Who is this? Is Brad all right?"

I put it on speaker. "Yes, Dr. Mitchell, he is fine. This is Detective John Stone, of the New York Police Department. I run a cold-cases unit at the Forty-Third Precinct. We are talking to your husband about the murders of Lea and Lee. I had a question for him, but he felt it was more appropriate that you answer it."

"What *question*?"

"Dr. Mitchell, do you recall a time when Lee tried to blackmail your husband?"

She was quiet for a moment, then, "Why, yes, but it was an absurd, childish thing. I believe he wanted something like fifty dollars a month, or a hundred. We all laughed at it."

"Could you tell me what happened?"

"Happened? Well, nothing *happened*. Brad called me to his den, where he was sitting with Lee. I remember Brad was laughing his head off and Lee was looking very offended." She started to laugh at the memory. "Brad showed me a couple of pictures on Lee's phone. They were of him talking to one of his colleagues at the university. Dr. Margaret Wagner. She now runs his clinic for him in White Plains. He told me that Lee wanted to blackmail him, and we laughed about it. Lee was very offended and ran off. Poor boy. He was having a lot of trouble adjusting to a new way of life. Do I understand you have reopened the investigation?"

"Yes, Dr. Mitchell. Somebody has come forward with new evidence, but please don't get your hopes up. The evidence is pretty thin. We'll be in touch."

I handed back the phone. "I'm sorry to have caused you distress, Dr. Mitchell. If something like this turns up, we have to look into it."

He nodded but didn't say anything. I glanced at Dehan. She shook her head, and we stood. "Thank you for answering our questions. If anything comes up, we'll be in touch."

"You're going to keep investigating? The other detective gave up almost immediately."

"I can't promise anything, but we'll have a look at it. Sometimes a fresh set of eyes sees things that weren't apparent before."

He lowered his eyes and bit his lip. "Sometimes I have wondered..."

"What?"

"That blackmail business. I have wondered sometimes whether he was not alone in that. Perhaps I should not have laughed. Perhaps I should have taken it more seriously. Perhaps there was somebody else behind it. And when it didn't work out..."

Dehan was frowning. "Have you anyone in mind?"

He heaved a big sigh. "It is so hard to be sure what my motivation is. Am I projecting? Am I jealous of Sonia, because he was close to her and rejected my paternal love? He was in touch with Sonia, a lot, you see? And I know he told her about his blackmail idea..." He looked at me hopelessly and spread his hands. "I don't know. I don't know if I have someone in mind or not."

"We'll look into it. We'll be in touch if anything comes up." At the door, with my hand on the handle, I stopped and turned back. "Dr. Mitchell, would you have any objection to our visiting the scene later?"

"I confess I can't see much point, but if you think it will help..." He shrugged.

When we got down to the street again, a breeze like a cold, steel blade was moving down Washington Place, stabbing people in the back, creeping through the folds in their clothes, and seeping in among their ankles to chill their blood. Dehan shuddered as she stepped out onto the sidewalk. She hunched her shoulders and moved toward the car with her hands in her pockets. I felt the cold creep into my shoulders and make my skin crawl, shoved my hands in my pockets, and jerked my head toward Washington Square Park. "Let's walk."

"Why? What's wrong with driving?"

"Come on, walking helps me think."

She fell in beside me, shaking her head. "You know it's cold, right?"

"Is he a good actor, or is he telling the truth?"

She shrugged with one shoulder. "He was pretty convincing."

"He has been in analysis for thirty years. Method acting and psychoanalysis are not a million miles apart from each other. They both involve exploring deep unconscious emotions, and tapping into them to understand them. A man who has spent thirty years studying his own unconscious emotions, and analyzing them, could conceivably give a very convincing performance by evoking the emotions he wanted to portray."

She watched her feet a moment as she walked and seemed to recite, "Indignation, grief, regret, confusion . . ." She paused. "When he called his wife, that could not have been rehearsed."

"I agree."

"In the first place, they had no time. In the second place, I can't imagine many women covering for a husband who is suspected of infidelity. I mean, nobody has a greater interest in knowing if he's been unfaithful than his wife, right? And if he had been unfaithful, Dr. Margaret Wagner has got to be a pretty good candidate as his long-term colleague and potential partner. She's also a looker. But his wife didn't seem in the least bit suspicious of her. Or him, for that matter."

I grunted. "I want to talk to Emma Mitchell, without her husband present, and hear from her what went down that day, and if there was any time during the morning when she was not with her husband."

She glanced at me. "We can get that from the file. But I really don't think she'd cover for him, especially as her daughter got killed in the same attack, and her son was driven into severe catatonic depression."

"I know." I sighed. "And I agree. But there is something about this that just doesn't hang together right."

We had reached Washington Square East, by the NYU Arts

and Science building, and crossed over to the park entrance. As we walked through the gates, she said, "We need to have a good look at the backyard. I mean, essentially, what we are saying is that, if Brad Mitchell didn't do it—and I don't think he did—there was a . . ." She counted out on her fingers. "Emma Mitchell, Brad Mitchell, Lea, Lee, and Marcus—that's five. So what we are saying is, there was a sixth person either in the house or in the backyard. That person got into the garden shed when the kids were playing in there, and killed Lea and Lee."

I nodded. "Testimony from Emma and Brad states that they were the only people there aside from the kids."

"But clearly, if Brad is not our killer, then there *was* a sixth person. So one of the questions we need to be asking is, how did that sixth person get in?"

We moved in among the crowd at the gate and then turned right, away from the people and in, under the trees. Dehan kept talking.

"Was he knowingly admitted? In which case, are they shielding him?"

"That seems unlikely."

"Yeah, I know, but psychiatrists and sociologists are all a little crazy, Stone, and we have to ask the question, even if we then dismiss it. Did one of them admit that sixth person?"

"Okay—"

"So we have to ask that, and we also have to ask, did one of the *kids* let him in, and the parents didn't know?"

"Which brings us to Mitchell's suspicion that Lee might have had some kind of accomplice."

"Right. Or, Lea or Marcus might have made a 'friend.' Sometimes the kids from these upper-middle-class families can lead very sheltered lives, and they can become really naïve."

I smiled. "So, if any of those scenarios is right, we are talking about a layout in the house and/or yard-cum-garden where the kids could admit somebody to the backyard without being seen by their parents, from wherever they were finishing breakfast."

She screwed up her face. "Yeah, from which they could not be seen, but close enough so they could also hear the kids scream. But then again, far enough away that by the time they got there, the killer had had time to get away."

As we pulled away from the crowd, she slowed her pace and linked her arm through mine.

I said, "I didn't get a chance to digest the file fully, but I do remember that they were having breakfast in the kitchen. It was a warm morning, and they had the kitchen door open onto the backyard. The windows were open too. I know they have a large lawn, flower beds, and trees. There is also a garage beside the house, and the shed is at the end of the lawn, up against some kind of a wall or a fence with trees."

"What's on the other side of the fence?"

I sucked my teeth and squinted up at the translucent green foliage above my head. "Another backyard, as far as I can recall. I'm pretty sure it's another backyard."

"So our killer has done one of four things." I was nodding, and she went on. "He has come through the front of the house or the garage, he has come over the walls at either side, from neighboring houses, or he has come from the neighbor's yard at the back of the house. Unless our killer is one of the neighbors, we can rule out opportunism. He was not strolling by and saw an opportunity. He actually intended to kill those kids."

We came to the arch, and I paused to stare at it with my hands deep in my pockets. It was massive, solid, immovable. The icy breeze crept down the back of my neck.

"Unless there is some form of access, like a gate, that somebody left open, or unless somebody left the front door open when they went to get the paper or something of that sort, it is really very hard to see how it could be anything but intentional, and premeditated."

She gave a small shrug. "Premeditated, or spontaneous but after a long period of provocation, buildup..."

I nodded. "It could be that." And after a moment, "So what are we saying then?"

She turned away, with her back to the arch, and stared away toward the crowds spilling out of Fifth Avenue.

"Dr. Brad Mitchell is very skilled at hiding his feelings and playing the part of the wise, mature psychiatrist, but in fact Lee's increasingly challenging behavior, his insults, and his threats had started to get to him. Something happened that Sunday. They were having breakfast, like they said, they heard screams or shouts . . ." She shook her head. "But they didn't both go to see what had happened. Brad went alone. Whatever he found in the shed was the straw that broke the camel's back. He lost it and killed Leroy. How Lea came to be killed as well, we can't know. Maybe we'll never know. But Brad went berserk and called his wife. When she got there, he told her he had found the scene like that and begged her to tell the cops they had gone to the shed together, otherwise he would immediately become their prime suspect, being apparently the last person to see them alive."

"Yeah, it seems to make a lot of sense, but only if you ignore the huge improbability of Mitchell killing his daughter, and we are back where we started."

"Alternative," she said, "it was Emma Mitchell."

I turned and frowned at her. "With what motive?"

"I'm just examining this from every angle, Stone, and thinking aloud. Motive?" She shrugged and turned to face me. "Motives to kill are not hard to find. Maybe she and Brad have an open relationship. Maybe she didn't give a good goddamn if he had an affair. Hell, maybe they were having a ménage à trois. Maybe," she said with more emphasis, "Emma is a shareholder in the clinic, with a vested interest in its success, and maybe that little brat Leroy was going to screw the project up for them by revealing that they were less than conventional in their amorous affairs!" She stuck out her hand and pointed her finger at me. "*Maybe*—and think about this—maybe his blackmail plot against Brad failed, exactly as they described it. So

Lee did some research and tried again, this time with Emma, and maybe he found that she had a lover at the Sociology Department. After all, Stone, Emma is just as liable to have an affair as Brad is."

"That is a hell of a lot of maybes, Dehan, with not a single shred of hard evidence to support the speculation."

"First, Stone, we need some kind of theory so that we can start looking for evidence. The guys in that initial investigation got all the forensic evidence there was to get. It led them to a blind alley. We need to think around this in a different way, develop some theories and see where they take us."

I sighed heavily and grunted. "That is a very dangerous way to approach a case, Dehan. You know that. The last thing we want to start doing is hunting for evidence, or tailoring evidence to fit our theories."

"I'm not advocating that. What I am saying is that the evidence we have from the previous investigation only takes us so far. So we need to develop some kind of theory, based on the evidence we have, and see if that theory takes us a little further."

"Okay," I said with little conviction, "like what?"

She spread her hands. "Look at the facts. It's like that Holmes thing."

"Eliminate the impossible and whatever is left, however improbable, is the truth."

"That's the one. Now, somebody killed those two kids, and if there was no sixth person in the house, there is no escaping the fact that it had to be either Brad Mitchell or Emma Mitchell . . ."

I stared at her for a long moment, then shrugged, and we both spoke at the same time.

"Or both of them."

FIVE

In the car, headed north through Manhattan toward the Bronx, Dehan called Dr. Emma Mitchell. She put it on speaker a couple of seconds before the ringing stopped and a slightly impatient voice said, "Yes, this is Dr. Mitchell . . ."

"Dr. Mitchell, this is Detective Carmen Dehan. You spoke to my partner a while ago . . ."

"Detective Stone, yes. What is it?"

"As you know, we are reviewing the murders of your daughter and your adoptive son . . ."

Dr. Emma Mitchell clearly didn't have a lot of time or appreciate those who would deprive her of the little she had. She sighed.

"You're quite right, Detective Dehan. I do know that. So there isn't much to be gained from telling me it again. What can I help you with? And please, come to the point. I am very busy, Detective."

Dehan narrowed her eyes at me. "We would like to see the scene of the crime . . ."

"Whatever for? We had cops tramping all over the house for days after the murder. They photographed it, measured it, scoured it, trampled it . . . What in God's name do you think you are going to get from . . ."

I'd had about as much as I was willing to take of Dr. Emma Mitchell and cut her dead.

"Dr. Mitchell, this is Detective Stone. I'm going to offer you a deal—"

". . . a *deal*?"

"Yeah, we won't give you advice on how to teach a sociology class, and you don't try to tell us how to conduct a murder investigation—or, for that matter, a cold-case investigation. It would be very helpful for us to be able to have a look at the house, the garden, and the shed. If you are unwilling to give us access, we will take due note of that and seek a court order. However, we would much rather have a positive, cooperative relationship with you."

There was a long silence. I wondered for a moment if she had walked away from the phone, but her voice came back with a peculiar tone to it.

"All right, Detective Stone. You've made your point. When would you like to see the house?"

"As soon as possible. How about today?"

"Today?" She sounded more amused than surprised.

"And I'd like to talk to you while we're at it, Dr. Mitchell."

"For sure. Will you want my husband present?"

"That won't be necessary for now."

"Say, three o'clock?"

"That will do fine."

"And, Detective, can you take me off speakerphone, please?"

Dehan raised an eyebrow at me and handed me her cell. I took it off speaker and held it to my ear. "Yes, Dr. Mitchell?"

"Will you be alone, or will your annoying partner be there?"

"We'll both be there. This is a murder inquiry . . ."

"Don't remind me, please. Very well, I'll be there at three."

We stopped for a coffee at the Shore Haven Diner on Castle Hill Avenue, and at ten to three made our way down to Turneur Avenue. The Mitchells' house was a large, two-story, double-fronted affair in cream clapboard, with gabled roofs and an art deco stained glass fanlight over the front door. Seven redbrick steps rose to a small porch with a white, wrought iron balustrade. There were two lawns at the front, with carefully trimmed orange trees, and a broad concrete path led to a double garage in back. We pulled up outside the white, wrought iron gate, and I saw that there was a cream Range Rover parked by the garage. Dehan raised an eyebrow.

"Who was it said there were no liberals left in New York, because they had all been mugged?"

I smiled. "It's a popular myth, but there are plenty of liberals left in New York, they're all just busy mugging other liberals."

The car doors slammed in the quiet street, and we crossed the front yard to climb the steps to the front door. It opened before we reached it, and a woman, still youthful in her late forties, leaned on the jamb and smiled at me.

"Detective Stone?"

"Are you Dr. Mitchell?"

"I am."

She held out a hand, palm down as though she expected me to kiss it. I ignored it and pulled out my badge.

"I am Detective Stone; this is my partner, Detective Dehan. May we come inside, Dr. Mitchell?"

She raised a mocking eyebrow. "So formal! By all means, come on in."

We followed her into what was not so much a room as a broad space that seemed to take up most of the first floor. There was a staircase that climbed up the left wall to the upper floor, and at the rear of the room a set of sliding, plate glass doors through which I could make out the luminous green of a lawn. In front of it there was a large dining table covered in magazines and newspapers. Bookshelves lined most of the walls, and to the right of the front door an eclectic cluster of armchairs and sofas formed a loose semicircle around an open fireplace.

She stopped and turned to face me. She didn't look at Dehan.

"So, what do you want to see?"

I glanced at Dehan. She said, "Where exactly were you sitting when you and your husband heard the screams?"

Emma Mitchell narrowed her eyes at me and turned on her heel. "We were breakfasting in the kitchen."

We followed her through a door to the left of the sliding doors, under the stairs, and into a kitchen, which, at about half the size of the living room, was still large. A window on the right overlooked a patio, beyond which a large expanse of lawn led to a pond and a row of cypress trees. Just beside them, in the far right-hand corner of the garden, there was a large, wooden toolshed. Flanking the lawn on both sides were rosebushes and tall, redbrick walls.

Inside the kitchen, beneath the window, there were two sinks and a marble work surface. To the left of that there was a door to the backyard. It stood closed. In the middle of the floor was a solid pine table, and up against the walls were a vast fridge, a sofa, a couple of scruffy armchairs, and a coffee table. Here too there were bookcases.

Emma Mitchell gestured with both hands at the table.

"That is where we were sitting."

Dehan stood and looked from the table to the window and back again. She moved to it, pulled out a chair, and sat down, looking over at the window again.

"This is where you were sitting."

"I said so."

"The table is in the same position it was in that day?"

Emma Mitchell sighed. "I told you, that is where we were sitting that morning."

Dehan glanced at me. "You can't see the lawn or the shed from here."

I jerked my head at the kitchen door. "That door was open?"

Emma sighed again, a little louder. "Yes, the door and the windows were open. I was sitting there"—she pointed at Dehan—"and Brad was sitting at the other end. We were reading the papers. I suppose the sounds of the children playing had become a kind of background noise, and we didn't really notice when it stopped."

She paused, leaned against the fridge, and stared down at the floor.

"Ours has always been a very peaceful, quiet home. Happy. We all got along very well. If there was ever any noise, it was usually laughter. Lea and Marcus used to laugh a lot. Nothing . . ." She looked up at me and frowned. "Nothing ever *happened*. Brad and I had the whole thing sorted." She smiled. "Our life was like a well-oiled machine. Everything happened as it should, according to what we had planned. That day should not have been different to any other. The silence that fell over the garden that morning, while we were sitting here reading, drinking coffee, should not have meant anything. It should not have presaged anything."

I rested my ass against the sink, and we waited. She looked down at the terra-cotta floor again and seemed to shrug with her eyebrows.

"It did, though," she said quietly, simply. "The first we knew was a terrible, shrill screaming. I remember it constantly, every day, at every moment, and every time I do, it seems to me that we sat there interminably, staring at each other without moving. And all the while poor Lea was in terror, being killed. And I was just sitting there.

"I ask myself, every day, if I had reacted sooner, if I had *done* something sooner, might we have saved Lea's . . ." She stopped and closed her eyes. "Might we have saved Lee's and Lea's lives?"

"What were they screaming? Were there words? Were they calling to you?"

"No." She gave her head a brief shake. "It was incoherent, like hysteria, shrieking noises."

I asked, "What happened next?"

She shook her head again. It was a gesture of bewilderment, still, after all those years. "I sat, like a moron, and watched Brad walk to the window and look out. Then there was another shrill scream. This time the hysteria was unmistakable. I recall it as though it were in slow motion. Brad turned and frowned at me. And I just frowned back." She raised her hands to her head. "I wish I could go back in time and kick us both, scream at us to get out into the yard and *do* something. But it wasn't till the third scream that Brad reacted and suddenly ran."

"What did you do?"

She looked surprised by the question. "Well, I went after him, of course."

Dehan leaned her elbows on the table. "At what point did you realize the screaming was coming from the shed?"

Emma Mitchell looked at her for the first time. She didn't answer straightaway.

"I suppose, when I went out into the yard. Brad was running for the shed."

"Was the screaming still going on?"

"No, it had stopped."

Dehan glanced at me. I gave her a small frown, but she went on. "So, you went for the shed because your husband was running that way?"

"Yes, I don't know what you're driving at."

I answered for her. "We're not driving at anything, Dr. Mitchell. We are just trying to get a clear understanding of what happened that day. What we would like to know is how your husband knew to run for the shed."

She blinked a few times, gave her head a small shake. "I have no idea. What a bizarre thing to focus on. Perhaps he saw that there was nothing happening anywhere else in the garden and decided it had to come from the shed. Or when he was at the window . . ." She shrugged. "You'll have to ask him."

I nodded. "I know this must be painful, Dr. Mitchell, but it would be very helpful if you could walk us through what happened next."

She closed her eyes and took a deep breath. After a second or two she released it, like she was blowing smoke from a cigarette.

She crossed the floor to the kitchen door and unlocked it. Dehan stood, and we followed Emma Mitchell out onto the patio. The sun was dropping toward the horizon behind the house, and the breeze had turned icy. I shuddered, and Dehan thrust her hands deep into her pockets. Dr. Mitchell hugged herself and stamped her feet, looking everywhere in the backyard except at the shed. I said, "You followed your husband across the lawn."

She nodded. "Yes."

She made her way across the lawn to the shed, and we followed after her. The door was closed. She reached for the handle but withdrew her hand before touching it.

"The door was open," she said. "A couple of inches. Brad grabbed it and yanked it. I remember he just stood there, immobile, staring down at the floor. I began to shout at him, asking him what it was, what had happened. He wouldn't answer. He didn't say anything. I came up beside him . . ."

She looked up at me. It was a kind of appeal, as though her face were begging me to tell her it had all been some crazy mistake.

"When I was beside him, I could see past . . ." She gestured with her arm, holding it straight out in front of her. "I could see past him, what was on the floor inside the shed. Lea . . ."

She squeezed her eyes and her lips closed tight, and she covered her mouth with the fingertips of one hand again. "Lea was lying on her back. Her throat looked black. And then I realized it was blood. Her eyes . . . Oh, Lord! Her eyes were open, and her head was thrown back so she was staring at me. And Lee, Lee was at her feet. He was facedown, with . . ." She made a strange stabbing, pointing gesture at her back. "With the knife poking out of his back. There was no sign of Marcus. I'm sorry . . ."

She stopped talking and covered her face with her hands. I stepped inside the shed, recalling the photographs I had seen in the file. It was as she had said. Lea had been flat on her back, with her arms by her side, her head toward the door, and a big, ugly gash across her throat. Lee was lying a couple of feet from her, kind of crumpled and twisted, with a knife protruding from his back.

Outside I heard a shuddering breath, then Dehan's voice.

"What happened then?"

"My memory is shaky at that point. I think I went hysterical for a bit. So did Brad. But he had at least enough presence of mind to call 911. Then there was a mad few minutes while we waited, both of us sobbing and wanting to go to them, but Brad kept saying, 'No, we mustn't disturb anything,' and we were both calling out for Marcus, but there was no sign of him."

I turned to look at them, from the blackness of the shed, framed brilliant against the green lawn. Dehan was asking, "When did you eventually find Marcus?"

She fiddled with her nails for a bit, with her eyes darting about the yard. Eventually she said, "I think I fell on the lawn. I remember sitting here"—she pointed to the grass at her feet—"and calling to Lea to please . . ." She bit her lip, and a tear welled in her eye and rolled down to the corner of her mouth. "And Brad was running around the yard, looking at the trees and the flower beds, calling to Marcus. Finally he came, just before the police arrived, and just kind of blundered into the shed, saying, 'This is the only place he can be!' And there was a tarpaulin over at the back." She pointed into the shadows where I was standing. "He went to it and pulled it back, and there was Marcus."

Dehan asked, "Did he say anything?"

She shook her head. "No, not a word. He was huddled in the fetal position, with his arms covering his face and his eyes tightly closed. He didn't move or say anything."

"What happened?"

"The police arrived, with the ME and an ambulance. They tried to get him to talk, but the medical examiner said he was in a catatonic state, which would probably pass in a few days. But it never did."

I asked, "Where is he now?"

Suddenly her face was hard as rock. "In his room, with his nurse, and you *cannot* see him!"

SIX

Dehan screwed up her eyes and sucked her teeth. She also hunched her shoulders and went up on her toes. When she came down, she said, "What is it, about our seeing Marcus, that you want to avoid?"

Emma Mitchell turned and stared at her with furious eyes. When she spoke, I noticed that her hands were trembling, but she spoke quietly.

"He is my son, he is all I have, he is hurt, damaged, and I am not going to allow you—or anyone else—to go barging in, dragging up that trauma..."

I interrupted her. "So he is not seeing a therapist."

She stopped dead. Her mouth kept working, but no sound came out. Dehan sighed.

"Dr. Mitchell, we are not here to cause you or your family problems. We want to catch the person who murdered your children and bring him to justice."

She emitted an ugly bark that should have been a laugh but had all the wrong ingredients. "Oh, please! Don't give me that New York's finest bull, Detective. I happen to have a PhD in sociology and I know very well how the New York Police Department works. Priority number one: close the case. It *really* doesn't matter if you get the right guy or not. The objective is to make up the numbers so that your political masters look good!" Her voice was becoming shrill. "Priority number two: *close the case!* And it *really* doesn't matter if you put an innocent person away—*especially* if he happens to be black! Because it is not about people! It's about numbers! Numbers that make the mayor look good! Numbers that make the senator look good! Numbers that make *your damned career look good*!" Now she was shouting, stabbing with her finger, her eyes bright with angry tears. "But the last thing you give a *damn* about is the devastated lives you leave behind!"

Dehan stepped up to her and took hold of her shoulders in her hands. She spoke softly, kindly. "Hey, Dr. Mitchell. You want to get your head out of your books and come down on the streets from time to time. You haven't got a monopoly on humanity. We're all people: the victims, the criminals, *and* the cops." She jabbed a thumb at me. "This dinosaur is working cold cases precisely because he doesn't give a damn whose toes he treads on or what politicians, red, white, or blue, he upsets or even puts away. You don't need to be an academic to have a conscience. Cops are like everybody else, good and bad, bent and straight, clean and dirty. Most of us are just doing a job, just like you.

"Now it just so happens you have, right here, two cops who are straight and clean, and our priority number one is to catch the bastard who killed your kids. But we can only do that if you work with us. So do yourself a favor, cut the crap and get with the program."

Dr. Emma Mitchell stared at Dehan for a long moment with wild eyes. Then she jerked her shoulders free from Dehan's hands, turned, and ran back across the lawn to the house. I watched her disappear through the kitchen door, and then she was gone. I turned to look at Dehan, who shrugged.

"She didn't tell us to leave."

I shrugged back at her and made my way past the shed to the wall of trees that formed the end of the yard. I examined them and walked the length of the row, from left to right, with Dehan beside me. They were dense, closely packed and entwined. Finally Dehan spoke my own thoughts: "It's impossible. They are impenetrable. The killer did not get into the yard through these trees."

"I agree."

"That leaves the walls either side of the yard." She turned, with her hands on her hips, and squinted at them. "What height would you say they are?"

I had already gauged them from the kitchen window. I said, "Nine feet, maybe a little more. And, see?" I pointed. "They're topped with broken glass. Not impossible, but difficult, very difficult. You'd need skills."

"Yeah." She nodded. "You're looking at using a ladder, putting some kind of blanket on the wall, and then using another ladder to get down. Unless it was one of the neighbors, I can't see anyone pulling that off in broad daylight on a Sunday morning without being seen."

I shook my head. "We'll talk to them, but you're right, it's just not a realistic scenario."

"Agreed. Which leaves us the front." She began to walk back toward the house, pointing as she went and talking over her shoulder. "There's a driveway down the side, that leads to a double garage. From the garage there is a path that leads to the kitchen door and the backyard. It's the only viable access."

We reached the kitchen door. I glanced in and saw Emma Mitchell sitting at the kitchen table with a mug in front of her. She was staring into it like a gypsy trying to read her tea leaves.

We moved on and followed a narrow path through a gate in a picket fence and out onto a concrete driveway. On our right was the double garage. To the left the drive led down to the sidewalk and the road.

"Easy," I said, "but the killer would have had to pass right in front of the kitchen door and the kitchen window. And—" I frowned and shrugged. "What's driving him? What's his motivation? I mean, does he arrive by car or on foot? What makes him stop and come up the drive?" I walked down as far as the sidewalk and looked up and down the road.

Dehan walked down as far as the blacktop, looked both ways, and then stood staring at me. She said, "He hasn't seen the kids. He can't see them from here. And either he doesn't know the Mitchells are at home, in which case he's taking a huge risk on a Sunday morning, or he knows they are home and doesn't care. He goes in anyway, which makes no sense."

"Also..."

She interrupted me. "Also, how does he know the kids are in the shed? Like you said, he can't see them. So what makes him go to the shed? He goes, bold as brass, right past the open kitchen door and windows, and goes straight for the shed. What made him do that? It makes you wonder, were the kids actually the intended target?"

I nodded. "That's a good question. I have to say, Dehan." I turned and started walking back up the drive, toward the garage. "I am not crazy about this theory. He comes up here to the gate..."

I stopped at the gate and looked into the backyard. The shed was not visible from where I stood.

"All I can see is the back of the house, the open kitchen, and the open windows. But I open the gate, and instead of going to the house, I cross the lawn to the shed, which we know was not open, but just a couple of inches ajar." I shook my head. "I cannot grasp what motivation he must have had to do that."

Dehan leaned her forearm on the fence and her head on her forearm. "Unless, as we said before, this was either an accomplice of Lee's in his blackmail scheme, or someone who had made friends with one or more of the kids and knew where they would be by some kind of prior arrangement."

I spoke half to myself: "Or the killer was already in the house. And round and round in circles we go..."

"Nah." I looked at Dehan and smiled. She had her lips pressed together and was shaking her head. "I just don't buy that. It doesn't make sense."

I opened the gate, and we went back into the yard and through the kitchen door. Emma Mitchell did not look up. I sat with my back to the sink, and Dehan took the seat opposite me. There was a moment of awkward silence. Finally I said, "Dr. Mitchell, you have to cooperate with us. The law requires it. But I don't want to approach this that way. If Marcus is ill . . ." She raised her eyes to meet mine, expressionless but somehow also menacing. I repeated, "If Marcus is ill, then there is absolutely nothing we will do without the authorization of a judge, or a doctor. But at the very least we need to know how he is. We need to know what happened to him, and we need to know who is caring for him."

Her answer was immediate. "I am." And then, "Me, and he has a professional nurse twenty-four hours a day."

Dehan frowned. "What about a doctor, or a psychiatrist? His father . . ."

"No!" She cut her dead. "I am his mother."

Dehan glanced at me. I said, "You said he was diagnosed with catatonic depression."

"He was. We employed several therapists, but they all had this same, *stupid* idea that the way to get him talking and responding again was to force him to go back and deal with what happened. It was the damn event that traumatized him! Why would we want him to experience it again, for Christ's sake? I will not have it! He has suffered enough, and I will not have some quack torturing him and forcing him to go through that hell again. *I* am looking after him, I am his mother, for God's sake. And I know what's best for my child!"

"Has he ever said anything, anything about . . ."

"No."

"Has he spoken at all?"

"No!"

Dehan leaned forward with her forearms on the table. "He knows who killed his sister."

Emma stared at Dehan with something close to loathing. "Well I hope he *forgets*! And then maybe my baby can come back to us. I wish we could all just *forget*! And I wish you would *go away*, and leave us in *peace*! We have been through enough and frankly, Detective, I don't want the killer found. I don't want the trauma and the horror of a trial. *I don't want* to look my little girl's killer in the face and relive the madness and the pain—the sheer agony—of seeing her lying there, dead! I just want to *forget*!" Her eyes were suddenly wild, and she stabbed at her chest with her finger. "I relive that horror every day! And it hasn't healed me! So why should it heal him?"

We sat in silence for a while. Dehan and I exchanged a look, and I nodded.

"Dr. Mitchell..."

She cut across me, speaking like an automaton. "Please, just go."

I glanced at Dehan again, and we stood. I took a card from my wallet and placed it on the table in front of her.

"Anytime, day or night. For your daughter."

"Go away, and please, don't come back."

At the door I stopped and turned back to her. She was still staring at her mug.

"I can't promise you that, Dr. Mitchell. We will be back, and we'll keep coming back until we catch the person who killed Lee and Lea. We are relentless, and you would be wise to cooperate with us."

We followed the path to the gate in the picket fence and the double garage, then walked down the driveway to my old Jaguar. We climbed in, and I sat for a while staring at the key before I slipped it in the ignition. Then I sat staring down the street at the plane trees and the ugly redbrick building on the corner. After that I stared at Dehan as she tied her long, black hair in a knot behind her head.

"I know what you're thinking," she said.

"Yeah?" I smiled. "I wish you'd tell me. All I have is a blank."

"You're thinking, it's impossible for a sixth person to have entered the house to kill Leroy and Lea by the back or sides of the house. So any sixth person must have come from the front, but that is so improbable as to be virtually impossible. Therefore, we are left with two possibilities."

"Therefore?"

"Indeed. Those two possibilities are, one, the Mitchells are shielding a sixth person who was there and killed the kids, which is also wildly unlikely, or two, it was one or both of the Mitchells."

I sighed and drummed my fingers on the walnut steering wheel. "I'll give you nine out of ten."

"It was not either of the Mitchells, Stone. There is no way either of those two killed their own daughter. I reserve judgment on Leroy, but there is no way they killed Lea."

"Based on what evidence, Dehan?"

She sagged, raised her hands, and let them flop into her lap. "Well, for a start, they alibi each other. Also, the way she told her story, she was reliving that event, Stone. You can't fake that kind of thing. That was genuine."

"That is a very dangerous way to investigate a murder, Dehan, and you know it. Basically you're saying she's not guilty because you believe her."

Irritation contracted her face. "Come on, Stone! You know me better than that! This isn't a court of law. It's you and me exchanging impressions."

"Okay, but as things stand, Dehan, you yourself have said that the only people who can feasibly have killed those children were the Mitchells. So, I have to ask you, in terms of hard evidence—something we can give the DA—what makes it impossible for the Mitchells to have killed their daughter?" She looked away, out of the window, chewing her lip. I added, "Or, for that matter, provide each other with a false alibi. You have to admit that her unwillingness to have anyone see, or even help, Marcus is suggestive to say the least. What did Marcus witness that she doesn't want him to talk about?"

She didn't look at me but just shook her head. "I don't buy it, Stone." Now she turned to face me. "I can't tell you why. I can't give you hard evidence. But I know, and so do you, that neither Emma nor Brad Mitchell killed those kids."

I turned the key in the ignition, and the big old cat growled into life. As I pulled away from the curb, she was watching me, with the dappled light from the trees touching her face. "You don't? Are you telling me you think one of them might have done it?"

"Not exactly, Dehan. I don't know, for a fact, with the same certainty that you have, that one or both of the Mitchells did not kill those kids. I wouldn't go so far as to say that I suspect that they did, but I am far from certain they didn't."

"But with what motive, Stone?"

"Blackmail?"

"But Emma Mitchell already dismissed that possibility..."

"Sure, but what happens if Lee insists? What if Lee had, as Mitchell suggested, an accomplice—an older person who is egging him on, pressuring him? What if he keeps coming back to Mitchell, telling him he has more evidence of his infidelity? Or evidence of some sort that could jeopardize the future clinic? And what if he will not desist? What if Leroy's emotional problems are eating away at their happy family? What if the Mitchells are seeing their idyllic setup slowly crumbling under Leroy's relentless assault?"

"Jesus, Stone..."

I drove in silence for a moment, with the leafy suburban street drifting by outside.

"It only takes the smallest variation in her story for it to work," I said. "The kids are screaming and shouting out in the yard. That's something Marcus and Lea never did before. Maybe Lee has hurt Lea in a fight, and Brad, who has had his fill of Lee, goes out into the yard and bursts into the shed. I don't know what he finds there, but it's enough to drive him into a rage. I don't want to dot the *i*s and cross the *t*s, because I am not proposing this as a theory. All I am saying is that given enough of the right provocation, I can see Brad doing something crazy and justifying it as protecting his family."

She puffed out her cheeks and blew. "Hell, I guess you're right, but . . ."

"I'll tell you something else I am not one hundred percent convinced about."

She turned to face me. "That Mitchell and Wagner never hit the sack together?" I nodded. "Yeah." She sighed unhappily. "I guess you're right about that too."

SEVEN

Dehan called the chief and told him we needed to talk to him. When we got to the station house, we climbed the stairs to his office and rapped on the door. Inspector John Newman was sitting behind his desk and laughed as we came in, as though we had made a comic entrance. "Ah!" he said. "The dynamic duo! How are we? John, Carmen! Please, sit."

We sat, and he sat beaming at us. I half expected him to get up and start mixing drinks. Instead he said, "What can I do for you?"

"This morning we received new evidence on the Mitchell case."

He frowned. "Mitchell, rings a bell..."

"2014, six years ago, a girl and her adoptive brother murdered in a garden shed in their backyard. Parents were inside having breakfast, but came out when they heard screams. They found the kids, one with her throat cut, the other stabbed in the back. A third kid, the girl's natural brother, was found hiding under a tarpaulin. He went into catatonic depression and has not spoken since."

He'd started nodding when I mentioned the kids in the shed. Now he said, "Yes, I recall something. You have received new evidence? Any good?"

"We're not sure yet, but we have spoken to both parents."

"They were, if I recall, academics? Liberals, active in the community..."

Dehan answered. "She's a doctor of sociology. He's a doctor of psychology. They are both Dr. Mitchell, so they never know which one you're talking to. You say, 'Dr. Mitchell!' And they both go"—she made an idiot face—"'What? What?'"

Chief Newman gave an indulgent chortle. "So what was the new evidence?"

I said, "That the adoptive child, Leroy, had been attempting to blackmail Dr. Brad Mitchell. He claimed to have information and photographs that showed Brad was having an affair. That information, at this stage, seems not to have much substance. But after talking to both the Mitchells, and the alleged lover..."

Dehan cut in, "Another doctor, also of psychology, she runs Brad Mitchell's clinic in White Plains."

I nodded. "Right, after having spoken to all three of them, and seen the house where the murder took place, the problem we have is this." I shrugged and spread my hands. "It seems the only people with opportunity to kill the kids are either Emma Mitchell, Brad Mitchell, or both of them. They also have means, and, if there is anything in this blackmail story, Brad Mitchell might have had motive too. The only other possibility is that there was a sixth person in the house, and for some reason the Mitchells are protecting him."

He blinked at me a few times. "Yes, I see. The two parents and the three children, and then a sixth person." He gazed at the ceiling a moment. "That's unlikely though, isn't it?"

Dehan answered. "I don't know if it's unlikely, sir, but so far there is absolutely nothing to indicate there was anybody else there, and we have no candidates to be that sixth man." She glanced at me and made a gesture of mild helplessness. "All we have is a pretty weak possible motive in the blackmail angle."

The chief gazed at her a moment and explained, as though to

himself, "It might just explain his killing Leroy, but it does not explain his killing Lea, his own flesh and blood."

"Exactly."

He looked at us both in turn. "So, what do you want from me?"

I answered. "We have one witness. Only one. And that is Marcus Mitchell, who is currently locked in his room suffering from chronic catatonic depression. He is not receiving treatment, and his mother will let nobody go near him but his nurses and his father. Apparently they employed several therapists in the beginning, but when those therapists tried to help him work through his experience, she fired them."

His eyebrows rose up on his forehead. "So she has him trapped in this catatonic state?"

Dehan said, "That's about the size of it. You have to wonder if she is just being overprotective, or if it suits her that the only witness is mute."

He grunted, picked up his pen, and examined it for a moment, then put it down like it was less interesting than he had expected it to be.

"So you want me to seek a court order compelling the Mitchells to give you access to Marcus."

I shook my head. "No, I want a court order compelling her to allow Marcus to have appropriate therapy, as dictated by the court, on the grounds that, A, he has evidence crucial to the investigation of his brother and sister's murder, and B, that his parents have proved incompetent in providing him with appropriate therapy. Catatonic depression is not an incurable disease. This happened over six years ago; he should at least be talking by now."

He drummed his fingers on the desk and chewed his lip.

"These are influential people, in their own way. They are active politically, behind the scenes. Don't be fooled by the fact that they live in the Bronx. They have friends in the liberal community who wield quite a lot of power."

Dehan gave a cynical grunt. "Beautiful real estate at a fraction of the price it would cost anywhere else, it bolsters your credibility as a person of the people, and at the same time, as the area becomes gentrified, you make a killing on your investment." She arched an eyebrow. "They may invest in Bronx realty, but they work and dine in Manhattan."

"Quite so. All right, I'll see if I can dig up a sympathetic judge. I might get you access, but for anything more there will have to be a hearing..."

I nodded. "I know. Maybe the threat of that will be enough."

"Let's hope so. I'll let you know as soon as I have an answer."

It was our cue to go, and we went downstairs and took a stroll through the cold afternoon light to the deli on the corner. We walked in silence as far as Banyer Place. Then Dehan stopped and said, "Okay, let's be a bit lateral." I made a question with my face and showed it to her. She ignored it and went on. "Let's just suppose for a moment that you were right."

"It has been known, Dehan."

She ignored me some more. "Let's suppose there is a connection between the killing of Leroy's parents, with a knife, like you said, and the killing of Lea and Leroy. What...?" She made horizontal circular motions with her hands and hunched her shoulders. "What *is* that connection? How does that work? What were you thinking when you said that?"

I smiled, and we started walking again. "It's not just the knives. Have you read the Brown file?"

"I haven't had time. We only picked up the case this morning, Stone."

"Well, I've only glanced over it, but a couple of things stand out as noticeable parallels. Obviously the murder weapon is the first thing. Statistically it is comparatively rare, but that Leroy's parents should be killed with a knife, and then he should, that is a statistical anomaly."

"Okay, that's the first thing, what else?"

We came to the corner deli and stopped.

"In both cases there were two victims, one male and one

female, and in both cases there was a traumatized child—the brother of the female victim—left behind."

She was frowning hard. She turned that frown toward the Bruckner Boulevard for a while and then screwed up her eyes at me.

"I mean, that's true, Stone. And it is weird."

"Remarkable."

"Okay, remarkable, but it doesn't *mean* anything. Does it? What can it possibly tell us about either crime?"

There was an icy breeze creeping down Fteley Avenue, and she stamped her feet and jumped up and down a couple of times. I shrugged and moved toward the deli door. "I'm not sure," I said, and pulled the door open for her, "but I don't buy that it's just a coincidence."

"You think it's the same killer? I thought it was established that they killed each other."

I shook my head and followed her in. "No, it's not the same killer, but I am damned sure they are connected."

We bought pastrami on rye and roast beef on whole wheat, and two double espressos, then walked slowly back toward the station house with the cold breeze creeping into our ankles and down the backs of our necks.

"The killings are connected somehow," I said.

"How? In what way? If it's not the same killer, *what* then?"

I didn't answer for a while, thinking over her questions. Eventually I smiled at her and said, "Maybe . . ." I shrugged. "I don't know. I can't put it into words yet. I guess I just think that, while we wait for the chief to get back to us, it would be a good idea to look into what happened in that first murder. Let's just say for now that the roots of the second killing might well be in the first one."

She gave me the kind of slit-eyed look that would have made a lesser man's toes curl. "If I said something like that, you would tell me it was woolly and vague, and to be more precise."

I wagged a manly finger at her. "And I would be right, little lady, I would be right!"

"Keep that up and I's gonna take my whip to you, boy."

"Ha!" We climbed the steps to the station door, and I stood aside for her to go in, muttering, "Promises, promises."

She dropped into her chair, retied her hair behind her head in a knot, and placed her boots on the edge of her desk. After she'd carefully unwrapped her sandwich, she shook her head at me before taking a bite and said, "I don't get it." She pulled over the Brown file as I sat and sipped my coffee, and started to read with her mouth full.

"Cherise Brown, married to Earl Brown. He's not a registered alcoholic, but widely known to drink heavily and regularly. Rap sheet with several charges for possession of marijuana, violence, blah blah. No regular employment. Word was he made his money selling dope. She worked the till and stacked shelves at Kmart. They had two kids, Leroy and Shevron. So he stayed at home, looking after the kids—for which read watching TV and smoking dope—while she went out to work, fed the family, and paid the rent." She swallowed, took a bite, and went on. "May 14, 2010, Cherise comes home early from work. It says here she was sick, but two gets you twenty she was suspecting something. You don't live eight years with a guy without getting a feeling for what he's about."

"You're probably right."

"So she walks in and she sees Earl raping Shevron. She's only six years old. Son of a bitch. And Leroy was watching. Later testimony from Leroy suggested that this had been going on for a couple of years, and he had been raping both kids." She paused and looked at me. Her eyes were bright with anger. "You know? Basically, in principle, I am against capital punishment. If you're going to kill a human being, it should be in hot blood. It should not be a cold, clinical social institution. That's in principle. But then you come across bastards like this guy, and it makes you question that. What use . . . ? I mean, what do people like this contribute to . . ." She sighed and shook her head. "Anyway, where was I?"

"Cherise had walked in on Earl raping the kids. But we know all this. We have already . . ."

"Shut up. So Cherise ran to the kitchen, grabbed a knife, and attacked him. They struggled, and the little girl, Shevron, tried to protect her mother. In the fight, either intentionally or by accident, Earl killed her. He hit her and broke her neck. Cherise then stabbed Earl in the back with the kitchen knife. But he must have been a pretty tough customer because it seems he took the knife away from her and stabbed her several times in the belly before collapsing. They both bled out just a few feet from each other, while Leroy watched them."

I grunted and asked, "Is that striking to you, Dehan?"

She stared at me. "What?"

"The way Earl died . . ." I shrugged. "The whole thing."

"Of course it is. What do you mean?"

I shrugged, shook my head, made a face. "I just find that very striking."

"Striking . . ."

"Yes, striking."

She scowled at me. "You're doing that thing again," she said.

"What thing? I'm not doing any thing. I'm just saying, it's very striking."

She pointed at me. "But when you say that, it means something. It means you have spotted something I have missed, and you're not going to tell me."

I was shaking my head. "It's not that simple, Dehan."

"But you know something."

"I'm telling you, it's not that simple."

"Son of a gun!" She stared at the perfect blue sky outside the window, and the motionless plane trees. "You *know* I hate it when you do that. We're supposed to be partners."

I shrugged and spread my hands. It was a gesture designed to convey helplessness. "It's nothing."

"Stone! What do you mean by striking?"

I sighed. "Look at the medical report. Where, exactly, was Earl stabbed?"

She leafed through the file and extracted the ME's report. She studied it a moment and said, "Half an inch above the heart, partly severing the right pulmonary artery."

"Right, with a broad-bladed kitchen knife. Now, if he was a really strong guy, or a grizzly bear, I could understand his turning on his wife, struggling with her and killing her, *if she had left the knife in his back*. Because that would have helped stem the hemorrhage. But, the problem is, he took the knife from *Cherise*. He didn't pull it out of his own back. That would have been physically impossible. Which means she must have pulled it out of his back after she stabbed him, perhaps intending to stab him again in a kind of series of hammer blows. But, if she had done that, if she had pulled out the knife after cutting his pulmonary artery, he would have bled out in seconds, long before he'd had a chance to grab hold of her wrist, much less fight with her and disarm her." I gave a short laugh. "I mean, just imagine the rate his heart was pumping in that moment."

She was quiet for a long moment. "You'd have thought so," she said at last. "But his prints were on the knife, and besides, the ME would not make a mistake like that . . ."

"I agree. Frank is much too meticulous and professional to make that kind of error. So I called him and asked him about it."

She frowned. "What did he say? And why didn't you tell me?"

"He said he really struggled with it. He told me it's one of those freakish things that conventional medicine cannot explain. Very, very rarely, a person possessed of an uncontrollable rage can keep going, keep fighting, even after they have sustained wounds that would normally kill a person outright. There have been cases of men receiving multiple gunshot wounds, or being stabbed several times in vital organs, who just keep going. There is apparently a huge amount of anecdotal evidence from various wars going back throughout history. The Vikings used to call them berserkers."

Her frown deepened. "So what made him think this dopehead was a Viking berserker, for Christ's sake? The most berserker thing this piece of pigeon's feces ever did was probably to turn on the TV for himself."

"I agree, and that's what I asked him. Frank doesn't make many mistakes, but what he said, basically, was that he and the investigating detective decided there was no other possible explanation."

"Oh, that's perfect. That's just dandy."

"As I said, Dehan, striking. There was, and I quote, 'nobody else who could have done it.'"

She was quiet for a long time, staring at me. Finally she said, "Yeah, striking, but what the hell does it mean?"

"That, Dehan, is the million-dollar question. What, as you say, does it mean? It *should* mean that Earl was dead *before* he took the knife from Cherise and stabbed her with it."

"Which, if you're right, and, annoyingly, you usually are, means that he couldn't have killed her . . ."

I nodded. "Which means that somebody else killed Cherise. Another striking parallel between the two cases: an unidentified *fifth* person in this case."

"And that would mean . . ."

"That Leroy saw it, and lied about it."

EIGHT

"Okay, Sensei . . ." She sat forward with her hands dangling between her knees. "I'll grant you I had not seen all that. I grant you also, it is not just the use of knives, there are too many parallels between the two cases for them not to be somehow connected." She shook her head a few times. "But *how*?"

I shrugged. "The obvious connection is Leroy, Lee."

She shook her head. "No."

"No?"

"No. It's not enough." She spread her hands and hunched her shoulders in a gesture that was unmistakably Latin, but also essentially Jewish. "What?" she said. "He was a collateral victim in the first murder, and a direct victim in the second. That does not in any way explain all the parallels. It does not explain how Earl survived long enough to kill his wife, or, if he didn't, who *did* kill her." She ignored my nods and went on. "It doesn't explain the use of a knife in both cases, and it doesn't explain the . . ." She faltered. "The coincidence of 'nobody else could have done it'!"

"Nicely put."

"Thanks, I've been working on it."

"There is another parallel which I think is important."

"Another one?"

"What you called the parallel victim. There is one in each case."

"No, it's too bizarre, Stone. There is no way of explaining that unless you start getting into all kinds of esoteric crap, karma, synchronicity . . . I mean, just what exactly are you driving at, Stone?"

I laughed. "Well, karma and synchronicity might explain a few things, Dehan, but I don't think we need go that far."

"What then? Are you saying the same person who killed Cherise killed the kids? We've been over that already."

I didn't answer. Something was nagging at the back of my mind. I said, "Where did Cherise work?"

"Kmart, on the till and stacking shelves."

"What about Sonia, where does she work?"

"I've no idea. What's her surname?"

"She's not married, so it'll be the same as . . ." I reached for my copy of the file, but Dehan was already saying, "Laplant, Sonia Laplant."

She dropped her file and rattled at the keys of her laptop. I read from my own notes: "One hundred Elder Avenue."

She typed some more; her eyes scanned the screen. "She works at the Bronx Rehabilitation Clinic, on Underhill Avenue. Why is that significant?"

"I don't know. It's a five-minute walk from Kmart. And isn't Elder Avenue pretty close to the Browns' house?"

"Uh . . . Wheeler Avenue, one twenty-six, yeah, just round the corner. Talk to me, Stone. What are you thinking?"

"I don't know. When I find out you'll be the first to know."

"That's funny, but not helpful. It's actually not all that funny either."

"We need to talk to Sonia again. She's told us half the story. We need the rest."

"Shall I call her at the clinic?"

"No, let's drop in unannounced."

It was less than a five-minute drive to the Bronx Rehabilitation Clinic, east along the Bruckner Boulevard and then over the White Plains overpass. The clinic was a six-story, redbrick cube set in its own leafy parking lot, with a blue awning over the door. It was subtle, but something about it said it didn't cater to Bronx junkies. It catered rather to those residents of the borough who would have lived in Manhattan if they hadn't been priced out.

We pushed through the glass doors and crossed a parquet floor to a high-gloss mahogany reception desk. There was a middle-aged woman behind it with huge brown eyes and very full, very red lips. She made a question with her face, brushed it with a smile, and waited.

Dehan leaned on the desk. "We'd like to see Sonia Laplant."

She did something in her throat that sounded amused, like "Hnnn . . ." and then added, "No can do, sweetheart. She ain't here. She gone out with Dr. Garrido."

Dehan showed her her badge and told her who she was. "When will they be back?"

"I have no idea, sugar. She's Dr. Garrido's PA, and he takes her most everywhere. Know what I'm sayin'? He's gone to buy some paintings for his office, and she's gone to help. Maybe she got a degree in art. I couldn't tell you."

"You know what gallery they've gone to?"

"Oh, I *can* tell you that. I got the brochure right here somewhere . . ." She pulled open a drawer and rifled through the contents. "Some place in Manhattan." She pulled out a glossy booklet and dropped it on the counter in front of Dehan.

Dehan read out the name. "The Searching I Gallery, I spelt with an *I*, not *E-Y-E*. Broadway and West Eighty-Fifth . . ." She paused, reading, then, "Opposite the French Roast restaurant."

I made eye contact with the receptionist and smiled. "Dr. Garrido is an art collector?"

She returned me the kind of smile that says, *You can believe that if you like*, and said, "Dr. Garrido likes anything beautiful, even if it is a little old."

Dehan snorted; we thanked her and left.

It was a twenty-five-minute drive via the George Washington Bridge and the Henry Hudson Parkway and then south to Broadway and West 85th. The Searching I Gallery was an ugly, gray, one-story cube that had been cruelly tacked on to a row of elegant, nineteenth-century brownstones opposite a French restaurant on the corner of Broadway. We found a place to park and walked, hunched into our shoulders, to the gallery entrance. The shadows were growing long in the copper light as we pushed in.

Near the entrance I saw Sonia standing with two men. One of them was by her side. He was of medium height and build, on the dapper side of elegant in an Italian suit, with expensively cut black hair swept back from his face. She was in a cream white suit, with a string of pearls around her neck.

Facing them both was a tall, willowy man in torn Armani jeans, with thick curly hair and a nose like a beak. He was gesturing extravagantly as he spoke, and wasn't aware—or didn't care—that his audience looked bored. Beside them were a couple of sculptures of unidentifiable shape positioned on stands, and hanging on the walls were canvases with pieces of mannequins attached to them, all with their eyes extracted and the sockets painted black. A large glossy sign by the door said that this was an exhibition by Zack Fuks, entitled *Blind Faith*.

As we approached the small group, the man I assumed was Zack Fuks was saying, "I adored her. It was an insane, wild, searching passion. I could not get enough of her. Truly? I think I burned her out, from the inside out. I was too much for her, and she could not take it. I used to call her my faith. My Faith. But she was completely ignorant of the *meaning* of our relationship. Do you understand? She could not *see* how our union of flesh and soul would lead to the fruition of my art. In the end, when she had nothing more to give me, she left. It destroyed me, but in my spiritual death, my art was born. That is why I call this exhibition *Blind Faith*. Who are you?"

This last was directed, with an arched eyebrow, at Dehan. Sonia was watching me with some alarm. I smiled at her.

"Hello, Sonia. I am sorry to interrupt you here, but there are some questions we need to ask you about your sister."

The guy who was obviously Dr. Garrido was frowning at us. "What is this? Who are you?"

I showed him my badge. "New York Police Department, sir. I am Detective Stone; this is my partner, Detective Dehan. We just need a few minutes of Ms. Laplant's time."

He turned to Sonia with a face like a pay cut. "What is this about, Sonia?"

"My sister." She said it like an apology. "I told you about her, and her son . . ."

He turned to me, and his expression had become incredulous. "You couldn't have found a better time?"

Dehan answered before I could open my mouth. She said, "We got the memo."

Garrido's frown deepened. "What?"

"The memo from the mayor, that said all homicide investigations in New York should be adapted so as not to interfere with Dr. Garrido's private life. You want me to tell you what we did with that memo? Or if you bend over, maybe I can demonstrate."

Zack Fuks placed his hands to his cheeks and gasped. Garrido's face flushed crimson. He opened his mouth to speak, but Dehan shut it for him. "Tell it to somebody who gives a damn, Doc. Two children were murdered; we're not going to pussyfoot around for your convenience. Live with it."

I turned to Sonia. "Can we talk to you, Sonia? We'll be as brief as we can."

She turned to Garrido. "I'm very sorry, Dr. Garrido . . ."

He scowled at us, then nodded at Sonia. "Of course."

She followed us outside onto Broadway, and we crossed West 85th to the French Roast restaurant as the sun was dipping below the tops of the buildings. We went inside, found a table by the window, and sat. A cute blond waitress joined us, smiling like she was really pleased to see us. She told us her name was Tracy and she would be our waitress today. We ordered three mineral waters, and she told us we could scan the code on the table to get a menu on our cell phones.

When she'd gone away, I studied Sonia's face for a while.

"Sonia, there are some things I don't really understand."

"What," she said and hesitated, "what sort of things?"

I leaned back in my chair and made a show of staring out at West 85th and drumming my fingers on the table. Then I held her eye and nodded. "Quite a lot of things. About the blackmail, the messages he sent you, his relationship with the Mitchells." I laughed. "The whole thing just doesn't seem to hang together." I sat forward and leaned my elbows on the table. "But what I am really interested in right now is exactly what happened on the day of your sister and Earl's murder."

"Well, it was just like I told you."

I shook my head. "No, Sonia, it wasn't."

Her skin took on a sickly hue. "I don't know what you mean."

I looked down at my hands and sighed, drummed a little more, and said, "We know, Sonia . . ." I looked up. Her eyes were wide. Her face was rigid. I waited, but she didn't ask. "We know there was somebody else in the house at the time of the murder."

Her eyes flicked over my features. She glanced at Dehan. She was like a trapped animal frozen by panic. Finally she said, "How . . . ?"

I gave a small laugh and shook my head. "See? That's the kind of thing I'm talking about. It seems to me that the question you would logically want to ask is, 'Who?' But you don't ask that. You ask, 'How?'"

She closed her eyes. "You're trying to confuse me and make me say things . . ."

Dehan said, "What kind of things, Sonia?"

Her eyes snapped open, and she pointed at me, echoing my

own words. "See? This, this is what Leroy used to talk about. Always pin the blame on the black person."

I asked, "Who's pinning blame on you, Sonia?"

"You're trying to trip me up and confuse me, and make me say things that you can use against me."

I gave my head a single shake. "All I'm doing, Sonia, is telling you that we know there was somebody else in the house when Cherise and Earl were killed." She swallowed. I went on. "Now you have taken that and run, and become very anxious, which makes me curious. And I would like to know what made you ask, 'How?' How what? How did we find out? Is that what you were asking?"

"No . . . maybe." She closed her eyes again. "I was shocked. I didn't expect . . ."

Dehan spoke softly. "I think you *half* expected it, Sonia. When you saw us come in."

"No . . ."

I interrupted her. "Here's another thing that I don't understand, Sonia. That photograph, the one you showed me of Brad Mitchell with Dr. Wagner. What I don't understand about that is why you didn't react exactly the way the Mitchells did when Leroy showed it to them." She didn't answer. She just stared at me. "You know what they did? Brad called his wife, and they laughed. They laughed in Leroy's face." I shook my head. "Why didn't you do that, Sonia?"

She frowned, gave her shoulders a small shrug. "I was worried. He's my nephew. I didn't want him falling into bad ways . . ."

I snorted. "You were that close?"

"We were very close!"

I barked a loud laugh. "C'mon! You were his aunt! You probably saw him once a month!"

Her face flushed, and her eyes were bright. "That is not true! I saw him most every day!"

"For what?"

She leaned forward now, real angry now. "Because Cherise had no car at that time, and I would take her to work and the kids to school..."

"The kids were not at school that day."

"Because that bastard Earl said he wanted to keep them off. He said they were not well."

Dehan's voice was heavy with irony. "And you and Cherise thought that was normal?"

"No! We did not! And that is exactly why she called me from work and said she was worried. She wanted to go back and check on them!"

I leaned forward. "And you told her not to worry. They would be fine. You left them in the care of that..."

She was shaking her head furiously. "No! No! No! *No!* I had told her from the start that she should *never* leave them alone with him! I had told her over and over that that man was dangerous! He was hurting those children. I'll tell you what I did. I told Dr. Garrido that I had to go out for the afternoon, and I went and got her and took her..."

She trailed off, but it was too late. I sighed and sat back in my chair. Dehan said quietly, "So there *was* another person in the house, Sonia."

She closed her eyes and echoed my gesture, sinking back in her seat. The smiling waitress came and distributed glasses and bottles of Perrier.

"Have you had a chance to look at the menu?"

I looked at her. "Just give us a few minutes."

She bobbed and went away. I turned back to Sonia. "You took her home and you both went in together..."

"No!" She shook her head furiously. "I left her there. She got down from the car, and I left. I had to get back to work..."

"Come on, Sonia! Time for the truth! You just got through telling us you told Garrido you'd be out for the afternoon. And you did that because, after eight years of this guy, you both knew him and suspected what was going on. That being the case, there is no way you would have allowed her to go in alone. It's over, Sonia. It is time to tell the truth. What happened that day?"

NINE

"They were really hard up. Earl hadn't worked for a long time. He made money selling weed, but he kept that for himself. They had sold the car, and every morning I went and collected her from their house, or she'd walk to my place. It was literally just around the corner. She worked at Kmart, and that was like two minutes from where I work, so I would sometimes drive over and we'd have lunch together. We always got on, even when we were small. She was a year older than me." She smiled. "But we always used to joke that I was the older sister. Usually I'd pay for lunch, and always we'd talk about the same thing, her relationship with Earl, how it was hurting the kids, how she should leave him . . ."

She sighed and shook her head.

"We even talked about getting a place together, but it never happened. A few times I would show her places we could afford, send her links by email. I was prepared to pay more than half of the rent just to get her away from that bastard. But I don't know if it was codependency, fear, addiction . . . I refuse to believe it was love. Nobody could love a man like that. Whatever it was, she could not let go of him.

"For a year, maybe more, before he died, she had started

confessing to me that she was scared he was abusing the kids when he was alone with them."

Dehan asked, "Did she say what kind of abuse she suspected?"

"I asked her, but she said she wasn't sure. The kids seemed to be scared of him. He was a violent bully, with women and children. He would punish them, hit them, shout at them . . ." She trailed off, then said, "I asked if she suspected sexual abuse. She said no, but I could tell by her face, by her eyes, that she had thought about it. It was . . ." She paused, staring out at the bright, cold street. "It was depressing, hopeless, struggling day after day, week after week . . . year after year, and realizing all along that the person I was fighting, the person I was struggling against was not Earl. It was Cherise. She was the person who was creating all the obstacles, making all the excuses. And all the while I was aware that a disaster, a catastrophe, was coming closer. It was as inevitable as the setting of the sun. As hopelessly unavoidable as nightfall."

She fell silent. We waited. Eventually I asked her, "What happened that day, Sonia?"

"I picked her up from home. When she came out alone, I asked her, 'What about the kids?' She said they were not well and Earl was keeping them home. I knew, by the way she said it, that she was worried sick. She was drawn, sickly, had bags under her eyes. I told her, let's take them to the doctor, but she said no, Earl would only get mad. It was best just to leave them. So we left, and I took her to work."

She stared at me with wide eyes, then looked at Dehan. "I couldn't work. I couldn't concentrate on anything. I was just sick to my stomach all the while. And I guess Cherise was the same because just before ten she called me. She was crying. She says, 'Sonia, I am going crazy. I am so worried about Shevron and Leroy. I think Earl is doing something bad to them. I think he's hurting my babies.' So I told her to hold tight, I was coming to get her. I told Dr. Garrido that I had a family crisis, and I went to get her."

Dehan asked her, "He was understanding about that?"

"He is a very good man. He was very understanding and told me to take as long as I needed. I collected her from the parking lot, and we drove back to her place." She stopped again and took a very deep breath. "I will never forget, as long as I live . . . I will never forget what I felt when she opened that door. You cannot imagine, unless you have experienced something like that, you cannot begin to imagine the sickening horror. I still remember, my skin went cold." She searched our faces by turns, seeking some sign that we might understand. "I felt sick. Hollow in my stomach. Your mind tries to tell you this cannot be real, but it is. He was there . . ." She gestured with her open hand, as though we could see what she was seeing in her mind. "He was there on the sofa, with Shevron, and Leroy was watching them."

"What happened?"

She sighed. "It was pretty much how the detective figured it. I was so stunned I didn't realize for a while what was happening. Cherise ran for the kitchen. She was hysterical, screaming. Earl kind of fell off the sofa, pulling up his pants. Then Cherise was there again, come out of the kitchen, crazy, with a big knife in her hand. I remember I screamed and told the kids to come to me. Cherise and Earl started fighting, and Earl hit Cherise. She was so crazy she didn't seem to notice, but he kept hitting her. And I was shouting to the kids to come to me, but they were just staring at their mom and Earl.

"Next thing Shevron kind of snapped out of it and ran at them. She started hitting and kicking Earl, telling him to leave her mom alone. He lashed out at her with his hand, grabbed her, but she wouldn't stop. It all happened so fast. Suddenly he had her—Shevron—in an armlock around her neck. I could see she was turning blue. I ran at him, but in that moment Cherise just kind of punched his back. That was what I thought. That she had punched him in the back, and I was surprised that it seemed to hurt him so much, because Cherise was not that strong. He staggered, and . . ."

She trailed off and started looking this way and that, as if she'd lost the thread of the story and couldn't find it again. I waited. She bit her lip and looked down at the table.

"What happened then, Sonia?"

She shook her head and shrugged. "What the detectives said. Cherise pulled the knife out and..."

"That's not true." She looked up at me. I repeated, "It's not true, is it?"

She faltered and looked away. "It's what the detectives said, and the medical examiner..."

"I know the medical examiner. I know him very well. Frank is a good man. He very rarely makes a mistake. But on this occasion he made one. He didn't know there was another person there. None of them did. So they came up with the only explanation they could. Frank knew it couldn't be right, but the only alternative was impossible. So he went with it and said that Earl had had some kind of berserker attack. But the fact is, Sonia, that when Cherise stabbed Earl, she cut his pulmonary artery, and when she removed the knife, when she pulled it out of his back, he would have bled out and died in a matter of seconds. There was no way he could have turned on her, disarmed her, and stabbed her repeatedly in the belly. He would have collapsed before he'd even grasped her wrist."

Her skin had gone pasty, and her eyes were moist, staring at me, defiant. When she spoke, her voice was little more than a rasp.

"What are you saying? Are you going to try and pin this on me?"

"No, Sonia. You know I'm not."

Her lower lip curled in. She bit it hard, and tears welled in her eyes. She whispered, "You can't. You can't, please, don't..."

"Cherise never pulled the knife from his back, did she?" She shook her head. "He fell to the floor, and, what happened? Leroy ran at her. He pulled the knife from his father's back and attacked his mother..."

She took a handkerchief from her bag and blew her nose, then wiped it, speaking as she did so. "He was hysterical. He just kept screaming, 'Daddy, Daddy . . .' He pulled the knife from his back and stood staring down at him. We were all just paralyzed. There was Shevron, and Earl, and it was kind of unreal. Then he started screaming, like he'd gone crazy, 'You killed my daddy, you killed my daddy . . .' He didn't say anything about Shevron."

She stopped, staring at nothing, staring at the horror movie that was playing in her head. She said again, very quietly, "He didn't say anything about his sister, only his father, and then he ran at his mother and . . ."

She covered her mouth with her fingers, and the tears finally spilled from her eyes and ran down her cheeks, shiny tracks of grief and pain, to the corner of her mouth. Now she turned to Dehan.

"How?" she said, in a strange echo of her first question. "How can a child do that? How can a boy . . . his own mother?"

Dehan reached across the table and placed her hand over Sonia's. I leaned forward.

"Sonia, we are going to need you to sign a statement. Technically, you suppressed evidence to protect your nephew. I am going to recommend to the DA that there should be no prosecution. I can't guarantee that she won't, but it is unlikely. Frankly, I think it would be a waste of public money, and an unpopular case."

"Thank you, Detective Stone. Honestly, this has been weighing on my conscience since it happened. I . . ." She shrugged. "I just did it without thinking, like I was in a trance. I took the knife from him, made him sit down, wiped the prints from the handle, and squeezed it into Earl's hand. When I heard the sirens, I just ran. I have never told anybody what happened that day. But I have dreamed about it so many times, had so many nightmares."

I nodded and after a moment said, "But I'm afraid we're not done."

"No." She averted her gaze. "No, I guess not."

"There is the blackmail." She didn't say anything. Dehan said,

"The photograph, Sonia, it was laughable. Why didn't you laugh? Why didn't you go straight to the Mitchells and discuss it with them?"

She shook her head but didn't say anything. I pressed her.

"I need to know, Sonia. I need to know exactly what happened with the blackmail. Because I have to tell you that right now, it doesn't make any sense at all."

A couple of times she seemed about to stand, but hesitated. She pulled her cell from her bag and looked at it, like she might be about to call somebody, then put it away. Eventually she said, "I was very confused. Unless you have been in a situation like that, you cannot begin to understand what it is like." She looked me in the eye. "I watched him murder my sister, but he was a child. He was my nephew. I wanted, God *knows* I wanted to forgive him. I wanted to wash away the past and see him become a happy, healthy young man." She looked down at her hands on the table. "Instead I saw his father's criminality, and weakness, creeping into his behavior, the lies, the deceit, the complete lack of any kind of moral compass." A look of disgust twisted her face. "The willingness to steal from the people who had willingly given him a home, safety, security . . ."

Dehan said, "You saw Earl in him."

"Yes, I saw more of Earl than of my sister. He had killed my sister in more ways than one. He had killed that part of her which he should have carried inside." She took a deep breath and let it out slow. "But even so, he was my nephew, my sister's little boy, and I had to do what I could to help him. So when he sent me the photograph"—she turned bitter eyes on Dehan—"I didn't really feel much like laughing. I was gutted, horrified. My first thought was to go and talk to Brad and Emma, but it's different for us. A white boy admits to blackmail when he is a child and everybody laughs. A black boy admits such a thing and he has the natural criminal propensity of his race. That wasn't something I was willing to burden Leroy with, so I tried to deal with it myself."

I sighed and rubbed my face. "Sonia, when you came to me it

was because you had seen in the paper that Dr. Wagner had been made director of Brad Mitchell's clinic. Now, stay with me here: the photograph Leroy sent you by WhatsApp was not, in any way, incriminating. It simply showed Brad Mitchell talking to a colleague. So there would be nothing odd at all about that colleague becoming director of the clinic." I sat back, watching her. She looked sick. "If that news article sparked a suspicion in you, it is because there was more to Leroy's allegations than you have told me."

"No." She shook her head. "Just that he was always saying that Brad was having an affair."

"Based on what?"

"I told you, he overheard things."

"And the best he could do was a photograph of two colleagues talking? What made him think it was Dr. Wagner? He must have spoken to dozens of women each day. Surely one of his pupils would have been a better candidate."

She was beginning to look harassed. "I don't know! I don't know what you want me to say! Those were the . . ." She stopped. Then, "Those were the things he told me."

I leaned forward and looked hard into her face. She avoided my eyes. "I need to see those other photographs, Sonia."

"There are no other photographs. I don't know what you're talking about." I drew breath to answer, but she glanced out of the window and said, suddenly, "Am I under arrest for anything, Detective?"

"No, Sonia, you're not under arrest, but we do need you to sign a statement."

"Then I am going to leave now. I have a job to get back to. A job I might well lose if you keep harassing me at work."

The door opened, and I glanced over and saw Garrido coming into the restaurant. Sonia stood. "I'll pass by the station after work and sign the statement."

She didn't say goodbye. She crossed the floor with quick steps and met Garrido halfway. She took his arm in a way that looked more matrimonial than professional, and they left the restaurant together. When they'd gone, Dehan turned to me and scowled.

"Where the hell did that come from?"

I shrugged. "I saw an inconsistency, and I picked at it. Something came out."

"Are you kidding me? An inconsistency? Seriously? She just confessed that she was present and saw Leroy kill his father!"

"I know. But it actually doesn't get us very far. The blackmail is still a problem."

I looked at my watch and raised a hand. She scowled harder. "Now what are you doing?"

"We're done for today. Now we need a roast chicken and a bottle of good wine. We need to talk this whole thing through."

She grunted and sat back in her chair with the look of someone who was relenting but didn't want to.

"Okay," she said, "but you are *not* to start cutting me out, Stone, or I swear I will kick your ass from here to Morris Park!"

I smiled at her. "Yeah, yeah, promises, promises . . ."

TEN

We started with a couple of dry martinis while we waited for the smoked salmon and avocado salad and half a bottle of Alsace Gewurztraminer. Dehan scorned the roast chicken in favor of an Argentine steak seared over hot coals, and I went with half a chicken roasted in a terra-cotta dish with baby onions, carrots, and potatoes. With that we shared a bottle of 2016 Domaine Jeannin-Naltet, Les Naugues Premier Cru. It was rich and bold enough for Dehan's steak, but had enough dark fruits for my chicken.

We didn't talk much while we were eating, beyond making appreciative noises about the food. When we were done we ordered a cheese board, black coffee, and a couple of old Bushmills, no ice. Dehan sipped her coffee and took a pull on her whiskey, then sat savoring it and watching me.

"How long," she said, "have you known or suspected that Leroy killed his mother? Because I have to tell you, Stone, it never crossed my mind."

I made a face that was somewhere between apologetic and pensive. "Pretty much since I read the report. We'll never know, and I am not about to call Frank out, but I think he dreamed up the whole berserker story to protect the kid. A black kid from a broken family in the Bronx, accused of killing his own mother, is going to have a tough time of it, whether he did it or not. Not only that, such an accusation could have seriously jeopardized his chances of adoption, even by the Mitchells."

"So, when you read the ME's report on Earl's wound?"

I smiled and shrugged again. "Yeah, the wound was pretty conclusive, but also, I mean, last man standing, right? There was nobody else left alive, so it had to be him."

She frowned. "Okay, that makes me feel pretty stupid. I should have seen that."

"Don't beat yourself up. You hadn't had time to read the report."

"Okay, but what about Sonia? How the hell could you have known Sonia was there?"

"I didn't, but it seemed likely." I cut a piece of Stilton and put it on a cracker, chewed it, and sipped some whiskey. "If you look at the report, which you simply haven't had time to do yet, you'll see that the only clear prints on the knife were Earl's, even though Cherise had stabbed him with it just seconds before he is supposed to have taken it from her. That doesn't make a lot of sense. Taken with the severity of his wound, and ignoring Frank's berserker theory, what we have is a situation where she stabs him in the back and he collapses and dies. Now, either she has removed the knife, or it is still in his back, but either way her prints should be on it, right?"

She nodded.

"Next, Leroy either takes the knife from his mother, or he takes it from Earl's back. Whichever it is, now his prints and his mother's should *both* be on the knife, but they're not. Only Earl's are. So we have to ask, how were Cherise's and Leroy's prints removed, and how did Earl's get there?"

I sipped a little more whiskey. Dehan watched me without speaking. I went on.

"At first glance, Leroy must have wiped the prints and pressed the knife into his father's hand, but I just can't see a kid of his age, in the emotional state he must have been in, driven to such a rage over his father's murder by his mother, thinking that coldly. Neither does it make a lot of sense that he would try to frame his father, when he has just avenged him by killing his own mother. That being the case, there must have been a fifth person there, a person working to protect the boy."

"That makes sense," she said a little gloomily.

"When I saw how close Sonia lived to her sister, and how close their jobs were, it just seemed very likely that that other person was Sonia. I applied a little pressure, and she came through."

"You say it like that and it sounds simple." She ate some Brie on a cracker and sat swirling the amber liquid around in her glass. "So how does this affect the Mitchells? You probably disagree, but I don't see how it clarifies the Mitchell case in any way? If Leroy killed his mother, who killed Leroy?"

I grinned. "Karma?"

"Yeah? Karma? That's about as helpful as a paper frying pan. Are you being facetious, or is there actually a thought in there somewhere?"

I cut another slice of Stilton, balanced it on a cracker, and inserted it in my mouth, then sat swirling the Bushmills. Outside the street had grown dark, and silent lights were sliding past, amber and red.

"What I mean is that—" I sighed and took a little longer to think it through. "That his own death, his own murder, may have been inescapably woven into his actions when he chose to kill his mother."

"Is that your brain talking, Stone, or the Irish whiskey?"

"A bit of both, perhaps."

"You're going to have to lay it out a lot clearer for me, big guy. At the moment it sounds like a Greek tragedy played out by black Vikings in the Bronx."

I laughed, then shook my head. "I don't know, Dehan. I haven't got anything you could call a theory. The possibilities are there, as plain for you as they are for me. All we can do is explore them." She stared at me, waiting, her eyebrows arched into a question that said, *So . . . ?*

I spread my hands. "Okay, so let me ask you this: What did Leroy take with him from his home with Cherise and Earl?"

"What did he take with him? I assume you mean something other than his pajamas. Uh . . ." She looked out at the quickening night and shrugged. "The first thing that springs to mind is his aunt."

"Okay." I nodded. "So run with that. How does his aunt lead to a kind of repetition . . ."

She sat forward. "Holy . . . !" I paused and waited. She said, "Did you see this? Is this what you have been driving at?"

"I don't know, Dehan. You'll have to tell me what it is first."

She narrowed her eyes. "Are you suggesting that Sonia killed her own nephew?"

I sighed and sank back in my chair. "Well, that is one of the possibilities, isn't it?"

"She said herself that she was struggling emotionally between guilt, the desire to protect her nephew, and her anger at the fact that he'd killed her sister. When you think about it, it must have been driving her crazy."

"It must have . . ."

"But what would trigger something like that, Stone? Out of the blue like that."

I took another sip of whiskey. "But it wasn't out of the blue, was it?"

"No." She shook her head. "It wasn't. She had made that huge sacrifice, allowed her sister's murder to go unpunished, saved him from the consequences of what he had done, and he shows his gratitude by trying to blackmail Brad Mitchell. She is suddenly overwhelmed by grief and regret and decides to set things right."

I thought about it. "Couldn't she have simply gone to the cops, as she did later?"

"Not without risking a prison sentence herself. She helped a murderer escape justice." She picked up her glass and set it down again. "Maybe she went there just wanting to talk to him. She arrived at the house and heard the kids playing in the garden. She went to the back, meaning to call him over and talk to him. Perhaps he didn't hear her, or ignored her, and she went to the shed..."

I nodded. "Perhaps. It's a lot of perhaps and maybes, though, Dehan, and it doesn't explain why she would kill little Lea. Seems to go against the grain if she's there to avenge her sister."

She grunted. "Stone, we have seen enough homicide to know that, unless you're dealing with a pro, people go a bit crazy when they kill. More precisely, people go a bit crazy just before they kill. We can't sit here in this restaurant and apply logic to what happened inside that shed when Leroy got killed. If she was there intending to avenge her sister, or seek justice for her sister, there is no telling what emotional state she was in. And if little Lea got in the way, or tried to stop her..."

She trailed off and shrugged.

I nodded. "Point taken."

"Just like Earl killed his own daughter."

I nodded some more. "I get it. It's plausible, but we still lack proof."

"The knife used in the Mitchell killing...?"

"Lea was killed with a knife that was kept in the shed for cutting twine, pruning, that kind of stuff. It was pretty sharp but had traces of rust, and that rust was found in the wound. That same knife was the one found in Leroy's back, very much in the same place where his mother had stabbed his father. There were no prints found because the handle had been wiped with paint thinner."

"And there was no other forensic evidence?"

"No." I picked up my glass. "A shed of that type is not ideal for recovering forensic evidence. There's a lot of dust, a lot of contaminants..."

"Plus a lot of people were moving about in there." She paused and sighed, gazing out at the cold Manhattan night. "I have to say,

Stone, it's hard to see a way forward. We have only one witness, and he's in a catatonic state."

She cut a piece of Stilton, popped it in her mouth, and grimaced.

"Why would anyone eat rotting feet?"

"It's an acquired taste."

She gave me a doubtful look. "I mean, even if we get the court order to be able to see Marcus and talk to him, there is no guarantee that he will talk to us."

"None."

She sipped her whiskey and leaned her elbows on the table, gazing at me. "What did that boy see, Stone? What did he see that traumatized him so deeply he stopped moving or talking?"

"He seems to have been a sensitive kid..."

"Okay, so a sensitive kid witnesses the murder of his sister and his adoptive brother, that is going to be traumatic, very traumatic. But, it is going to be that much more traumatic if it's his dad, or, let's face it, his mother, who strikes the blow."

I grunted and sliced at the Brie.

"You were against that idea this afternoon. Are we now saying our suspect pool is both the Dr. Mitchells and Sonia?"

She ran her fingers through her hair and looked cutely frazzled. "I know. I know, but it has to be one of those three, doesn't it?"

I pierced the Brie with my knife and looked her in the eye.

"There is somebody we have been overlooking, Dehan, and I don't know why."

She frowned. "Who?"

"Dr. Wagner."

"Hell. She had as much to lose from Leroy's blackmail as the Mitchells did. It may have struck the Mitchells as funny, but it probably didn't strike her as funny at all."

"It's a possibility."

"How would that work?"

I signaled the waiter to bring us another couple of whiskeys.

"How would that work?" I thought about it. "Assuming there is more to the relationship between Wagner and Mitchell than just work, he would tell her about Leroy. He'd tell her they managed to laugh it off but that they need to be careful with the kid." I cut a slice of Wensleydale and put it in my mouth, savoring the blueberries in the creamy cheese. Then I pointed at Dehan. "She would advise him to get rid of the kid, send him back to the orphanage, something of that sort. He does not see it as that important. He thinks the kid is just playing, he's not serious. So Wagner decides to take matters into her own hands."

She made a doubtful face. "It's feasible, but based on . . ." She spread her hands and shrugged.

I laughed. "Like everything else, it's based on the fact that we have a pool of suspects so small it barely exists at all, plus a total dearth of forensics and witnesses. Our logical process in this case seems to be, 'Somebody had to do it, these are the only people with opportunity, it must be one of them.'"

She nodded. "That *is* our process of deduction in this case, Stone. It's not good enough, but it's all we've got."

The waitress brought our whiskeys, and I asked for the check. When she'd gone, I took a sip and said, "Well, I think it's got us about as far as it can. If we are going to put together a case the DA can use, we need to start to gather either witness testimony or forensic evidence." I smiled, a little ruefully. "Or preferably both."

"That would be nice."

We stepped out into the cold night. An icy breeze was creeping down Broadway, making you shudder and shiver as it felt its way down collars and into ankles. Dehan came close and put her arms around my waist. I shared my coat with her and hailed a cab.

ELEVEN

Eight o'clock the next morning the call came from the chief while we were having breakfast.

"John, good morning, I hope I haven't woken you."

"No, sir, we've been up for a while. Any news on the court order?"

"I spoke to Judge Henderson. He's usually pretty sound. He has signed an order for you to have access to the boy for as long as you need, reviewable after a week. Obviously that is subject to normal lawful limitations."

"A week?" I put the phone on speaker and laid it on the table. Dehan froze with a forkful of bacon and eggs halfway to her mouth and stared at me. "That won't be much use, sir. The kid has been catatonic for about six years. We not only need access to him, we need to get him into therapy."

"Quite so, John, but as he explained to me, he can't make an order as sweeping and far reaching as that without a hearing. He would have to make the child—though he is in fact a young man now—a ward of court, when the boy already has responsible parents. He can't do that without very good reason, reason which must be heard and proven in open court."

"So where do we go from here?"

"The first step, John, is for you to collect the order, deliver it to the Mitchells, and see the boy. On the strength of what you observe there, we may or may not be able to apply for a hearing in which we request the court make an order requiring the parents to provide the boy with appropriate therapy, to be approved by the court."

I sighed and rubbed my face. "Okay, thank you, sir. We're on our way."

Dehan mopped the egg from her plate with a hunk of bread and spoke through a mouthful of breakfast.

"Pick up the order, go talk to Marcus, then pick up your car."

"Makes sense to me."

But it didn't work out that way. Halfway down Morris Park Avenue, with Dehan in the driver's seat of her Toyota Corolla, my cell rang. It was Maria, the desk sergeant at the station.

"John, you and Carmen need to get to 1001 Elder Avenue, corner of Bruckner Boulevard."

I frowned. Dehan glanced at me. "What's it about, Maria? We're on our way to the station. We need to collect an order from the chief..."

She cut across me. "I'm thinking this has priority, handsome. Sergeant Gunther responded to a 911 just twenty minutes ago. He called in and told me to get you. He said he thought it was your case."

I was visualizing the map in my head and sighed. "Thanks, Maria."

I hung up and put my phone away. To Dehan I said, "Elder and Bruckner."

I heard her swear softly. We followed Morris Park to the end, crossed the tracks, and took the Bronx River Avenue to East 173rd and Boynton Avenue. At the end of Boynton we found the end of Elder Avenue, the boulevard, two patrol cars, an ambulance, a crime scene van, and Frank the ME's beaten-up old Ford. They were all grouped around number 1001, with the blue tape hanging listless in the cold morning air.

Dehan parked beside the ME's car, and we climbed out. Sergeant Gunther, a tall platinum blond with a face like a slab of chiseled concrete, came down the dogleg iron steps from the front porch to meet us.

"Detectives, you're looking at a cold case about the Mitchell kids, right? I heard yesterday the kid's aunt had come in to talk to you about it."

I nodded. "Yeah." I pointed at the house. "This is the aunt, right?"

"I think so, but you'd better have a look."

Dehan asked, "What happened?"

"She's in the living room. Her boss is there. She didn't turn up for work, and he came to see if she was okay." He arched his brows. "Apparently he has a key."

"Thanks, Gunther, good call."

He raised the tape, and we ducked under it, then climbed the eleven metal steps that described a right angle up to the front door.

The living room was small. It was full of two men and a woman dressed in white plastic who were meticulously examining everything and taking photographs of what they examined. As well as them there was Sonia, lying on her back on the floor. She no longer looked elegant or desirable. Her left leg was bent at an odd angle. Her right was straight. She was wearing red shoes and a red dress. Her arms were straight by her side, and her eyes were goggling at the ceiling. Frank was hunkered down beside her, making the place look cramped. He glanced up at us but said nothing and looked back at Sonia. I said, "I saw her yesterday morning. Dehan and I both saw her yesterday afternoon. She's Sonia Laplant."

He cleared his throat and stood, pulling off his plastic gloves. "That's what her ID says. A tragic, blighted family. Her nephew, as you know, was the boy killed in the Mitchell case, which you are currently warming over."

Dehan asked, "How'd she die?"

"She was shot; in the chest, at short range. Obviously I'll be able to tell you more once I get her to the lab, but prima facie, it seems the first shot went in straight, horizontal. The killer stood thus..."

He stood a couple of yards from the soles of Sonia's feet and thrust out his arm in front of him.

"So the killer is probably a little shorter than me, maybe five-ten or five-eight. The first shot punches into her chest and makes her fall back. Then he closes in and stands over her, and the next two bullets enter her chest at an angle of about forty or forty-five degrees. He is standing roughly at her feet. He is not a good shot, because only one of the bullets hits the heart. Two others puncture the lungs, and a fourth misses altogether and grazes her shoulder to strike the floor. The erratic shooting is consistent with a trembling hand. Joe has the slug. It's a .22." He paused, still staring down at the body. "Such a shame." And then, "Joe is upstairs. He'll tell you there are no casings, so it was probably a revolver. Twenty-two revolver, the perfect murder weapon."

He turned to Dehan, as though she had asked a question. "There is rarely an exit wound with a .22, so the slug stays inside, ricocheting and causing more damage than a mere entry wound. Plus there are no casings for people like Joe to find and lift prints from. They are small and thus easy to conceal, but with a Smith and Wesson 617, for example, or the Ruger, you're looking at ten rounds in the cylinder, as opposed to just five or six in a larger caliber. Very handy."

I turned to Gunther. "Where's Garrido?"

"The boss? He's in the kitchen, back of the house."

We stepped into the small kitchen. Dr. Garrido was sitting at an imitation pine table. He looked up at us as we entered. There was a kind of mindless reproach in his eyes. He was drawn and a sickly gray color. There was a female police officer sitting at the table with him scribbling in a pad.

"Dr. Garrido." He nodded once. I went on, "We met briefly yesterday."

He pointed toward the living room, and his voice wavered when he spoke. "Did you do this? Did you make this happen?"

I frowned. "What are you talking about, Dr. Garrido?"

"Butting in, stirring things up, asking questions. I was trying to make her forget, and you come and bring it all back. I told her to leave it be!"

Dehan replied. "You have a family, Dr. Garrido?"

His voice was defensive when he said, "Yeah. What's it to you?"

"You have kids?"

"What of it?"

"If they were murdered, would you prefer the police refused to investigate, in case somebody else got hurt?"

Before he could answer I asked him, "Why are you here, Dr. Garrido?"

He erupted, "I did not kill Sonia, if that's what you're implying!"

"That's not what I'm implying." I pulled out a chair and sat at the table. Dehan leaned against the doorjamb. "I'm not implying anything. I am asking you what you are doing here."

"I already told your sergeant, and I have just told your officer here. When Sonia didn't turn up for work, I came to see if she was all right. I have witnesses who will tell you . . ."

Dehan cut him short. "You have keys to all your employees' houses?"

He faltered, and I asked, "See, that's what I meant by, what are you doing here? Correct me if I'm wrong, but I think most bosses would phone, or at most knock on the door. I don't think many of them would let themselves in with their own key."

He sighed and sagged, then rubbed his face with his hands. "Sonia has been my personal assistant for a long time, and we have become very close."

"How close, Dr. Garrido?"

He took a deep breath and puffed out his cheeks. He was obviously in a lot of emotional pain. I leaned forward with my elbows on the table. "We're not here to judge anybody. What you and Sonia did as consenting adults is none of our business. If it had nothing to do with her murder, then I, frankly, don't want to know about it. But if you try to hide it from me, and I don't know if it's relevant or not, then I am going to have to leave no stone unturned until I find out the truth. So believe me, if your affair with Sonia has nothing to do with her death, your best plan is to talk to me."

He let me finish without looking at me. Then, after a moment, he started to talk.

"Sonia and I have been . . . close, for many years. It suits . . . suited us both. My wife and I stopped being in love a long time ago, but we agreed to stay together for the sake of the children. For her part, Sonia didn't want us to live together. After we started seeing each other, I offered to get a divorce so we could be married. Personally I would have preferred it. I'm more traditional in that way. But Sonia said she preferred living alone, in her own space. We actually fought about it, years ago, right at the beginning, but eventually"—he shrugged—"we just settled into a comfortable rhythm. Sometimes I would stay the night. My wife knew about it, but she never asked questions. It seemed to work. Sonia and I even talked about retiring together. Now that will never happen . . ." His bottom lip curled in, and tears welled in his eyes. He stared at me with wild, injured eyes, then up at Dehan by the door. "Why? Why would somebody do this?"

"When did you last talk to Sonia, Dr. Garrido?"

"Last night, about eleven thirty, or shortly before twelve. We didn't talk. I sent her a WhatsApp wishing her good night."

"Did she reply?"

"Yes." He frowned at me. "It struck me as an odd message at the time. She said, 'You are too good. Sonia doesn't deserve you.' That wasn't like her, saying that, and in the third person like that. There was no false modesty or cute fishing for compliments with her. She was very direct and very honest." His face crumpled, and there was a madness in his gaze. "You don't think that message was from . . . ?"

Dehan had already gone and was crossing the living room, shouting, "Joe! Joe!"

I shook my head. "I don't know, Dr. Garrido, but we'll check, and I'll let you know what the lab says about her phone. Now, I need you to think carefully about this before you answer. Is there anything, anything at all, that you can think of that struck you as odd or unusual in her behavior recently? Anything she did or said, anybody she saw . . ."

He took a long time to answer. When he finally did, he made a couple of false starts. "She . . ." He gave his head a small shake and frowned. "About a month ago? She started talking again about her sister, and her nephew, Lee."

I raised an eyebrow. "Lee?"

He looked surprised. "Yeah, Lee, the boy whose murder you're investigating."

"I thought she called him Leroy."

"No, that's what his parents called him. She never liked it. It was Sonia who told the Mitchells his nickname was Lee."

I thought about that a moment, then made a mental note. To Garrido I said, "So what kind of things was she saying about them? What was it she was remembering?"

He looked me in the eye. "I didn't like it much, to be honest. She kept talking about Brad Mitchell. She called him a skunk. Said he'd betrayed his wife, how he deserved to be exposed for what he was. She even went so far as to say she believed he might have killed his own daughter, as well as Lee."

"What made her say that? Did she give you any idea of what brought this on?"

"No, it was sudden. One day she just seemed real mad . . ."

"That was all a month ago?"

"More or less, yeah. I told her if she really believed it, and it was affecting her so much, she should go to the cops."

"Was this when she saw the article in the paper? The one about the Mitchell Clinic in White Plains."

"Uh . . ." He made a dubious face and stared up at the ceiling. "Uh . . ." He shook his head. "No, it was kind of the other way. I showed her the article because she had been talking so much about Mitchell. Otherwise I would probably never have even noticed it. I saw it and showed it to her, and she got pretty mad. So I told her, 'For God's sake, go to the cops and get this off your chest!' So she did."

"Okay." I nodded, thinking. "I appreciate your candor, Dr. Garrido. You are familiar with the house. Are you aware of anything having been disturbed, turned over, missing?"

"No, it was the first thing I checked after I called the cops."

"Fine. We'd be grateful if you could drop by the station later today to read and sign your statement." I moved to get up but stopped. "Did Sonia have a computer at work?"

"No." He shook his head. "She used her own laptop."

"Okay, good." I glanced at the uniform. "You done?"

She nodded. "Sure."

"Dr. Garrido, you can go home now. Be with your family, get some rest. We'll be in touch."

He left, and I went to look for Dehan. She was upstairs in the master bedroom talking to Joe. She turned to me as I came in.

"There's no sign of forced entry."

"Yeah, and Garrido says there's no sign that anything was stolen."

"So she let whoever it was in, probably knew them, and they came for the sole purpose of killing her."

"It looks that way."

She nodded. "Her cell has been dusted. So far prints show one principal user."

Joe added, "Which we can assume to be her. But there are smudges, as though somebody had used it who was wearing gloves. We'll give it a full analysis at the lab, and I'll let you know."

"Sure, good. I also want every other form of communication in the house bagged and gone over with a fine-tooth comb: tablet, laptop, desktop, whatever else you can find. I want to know every message she sent and received over the last four to six weeks: Facebook, Twitter, WhatsApp, email—everything. I want to know who was talking to her, and I want to know what they said to her a month ago."

"Okay, noted." He smiled. "So unless there is something else, get off my crime scene and let me do just that."

We thanked him, and Dehan followed me downstairs. "Feel like sharing, Sensei?"

"Sure." We stepped out of the house onto the porch and followed the dogleg steel stairs down to the front yard and the sidewalk. There I leaned my ass on the hood of her small car and looked up at her. The wind dragged a few strands of her hair across her face. She brushed them away and looked astonishingly natural and beautiful doing it. For a moment I was distracted, wondering, not for the first or last time, how I had wound up so lucky. She said, "So?"

I smiled. "About a month ago, somebody said something to Sonia which made her so mad she decided she wanted to expose Dr. Brad Mitchell for, and I quote, 'what he was.'"

"And what was, or is, he?"

"According to her, a man capable of killing his own daughter, as well as Leroy."

"Huh..."

"And, curiously enough, this anger against Brad Mitchell started *before* she saw the article about the clinic and Dr. Wagner. In fact, it was that anger which prompted her to bring the article to me. I want to know what sparked that anger, and why she didn't tell me about it when she came to see me. What she told me was that the Mitchells were good people, and Lee should have been grateful to them."

She watched me for a moment, then said, "I know that look on your face, Stone. You think you already know what made her mad."

"Do I? Maybe. I don't know. Maybe not. I'm not sure."

She pointed her finger at me. "You better not be cutting me out, Stone! It makes me really mad when you do that! I am *not* Dr. John Watson, here to make your brilliance shine brighter by contrast!"

I frowned and gave my head a small shake. "That is such a hurtful, unkind thing to say, Dehan."

"Jackass!" She made for the driver's side and opened the door, then pointed at me across the roof. "Sofa. Sofa tonight."

"More unkindness."

"Sofa!"

"You'll come looking for me when the night grows cold and dark. You'll see."

"Sofa!"

And she slammed the door.

TWELVE

The chief was watering the bonsai tree on his windowsill when we entered his office. Dehan stood staring at the tree as he gestured us to the chairs at his desk. I always had the feeling with Inspector John Newman that instead of talking to the senior officer at a police precinct in the Bronx, I was visiting a kindly but absentminded uncle somewhere in deepest New England.

Dehan pointed at the small tree. "Japanese, right?"

"Indeed, Carmen. In fact, the term 'bon-sai' is Japanese and means literally, 'planted in a pot' or 'planted in a container.' The art of cultivating bonsai trees originated in ancient China, but was brought to its highest artistic expression in Japan, among Zen Buddhists."

"And the idea," she said, "is to care for it and tend to it, so it doesn't grow?"

He roared with laughter, sat in his chair chuckling, and nodded. "Yes, that is precisely it, yes." He chortled some more and, as we sat, asked, "So, what can I do for you?"

I told him, "We've just come from Sonia Laplant's house, sir. Her nephew, you recall, was Leroy Brown, the boy adopted by the Mitchells..."

"Ah, yes, the Mitchell case you're working on."

"Well, Sonia Laplant has been murdered, sir. Three shots to the chest with a .22. There was no sign of forced entry or robbery, attempted or otherwise. So it seems reasonable to assume she allowed her killer in, he was known to her, and was there for the purpose of killing her. That being the case, sir, it also seems reasonable to assume the murderer has something to do with our investigation."

He made a noise that suggested he thought I was making assumptions I wasn't entitled to. Dehan pushed up her sleeves and tied her hair behind her neck as she spoke.

"Here's the thing, sir. Sonia was involved in a long-term relationship with Dr. Garrido, the director of the Bronx Rehabilitation Clinic. He was the one who drew to her attention the article about Dr. Brad Mitchell opening a new clinic in White Plains, and installing Dr. Wagner as the director."

He raised a hand. "As I recall, you told me the boy Leroy wanted to blackmail Dr. Mitchell because he believed he and Wagner were having an affair."

Dehan answered. "That's right. And Brad Mitchell told us that he had a feeling Sonia might have been involved in that blackmail attempt. Now, what's interesting about her murder, sir, is that according to Dr. Garrido, Sonia had become obsessed with Brad Mitchell some three or four weeks *before* Garrido showed her the article about the clinic."

"Obsessed in what way?"

"Angry, accusing him of killing the kids..."

I stepped in. "Something happened, about a month ago, that triggered this obsession in Sonia. According to Garrido, suddenly Brad Mitchell was all she could talk about. She apparently called him a skunk and stated that he had betrayed his wife. She said he deserved to be exposed for what he was, a man capable of killing his own daughter, as well as Lee. Now, I think it is very important that we find out what it was that triggered that obsession a month ago. Because it is that obsession that brings her to the article—Garrido only showed it to her *because* she was talking about him so much—and with the article, to me. And just twenty-four hours after she comes to me with that article, she is murdered."

He made a deep, rumbling "hmmm . . ." sound. Then added, "Something tells me you are going to ask me to authorize something controversial."

"I am going to go through all her emails and every other form of communication she had that I can lay my hands on, focusing on the period four to five weeks ago."

"Good."

"I also plan to go through her financials. I don't know exactly why, but I need to know what she was doing and what was going on a month ago. Did she go somewhere, did she have an extra-large expense or receipt . . . ?" I shrugged. "Something happened that turned her against Dr. Brad Mitchell. We don't know what. But I have a pretty strong hunch we'll find out from her communications and her bank account."

He arched an eyebrow at me and rumbled. "I suppose you're right. But you are of course at liberty to do both those things. What do you want from me?"

"I want to look at Dr. Brad Mitchell's communications and his financials too, and his wife's."

"Good heavens, John! On what grounds? They are the victims, for heaven's sake."

"Are they? There is one pretty persuasive theory—held by Sonia Laplant, incidentally—that says Leroy was blackmailing Brad Mitchell, and Brad Mitchell killed him for it."

He frowned a frown that was almost a scowl. The chief didn't like ideas that involved kindly middle-class fathers killing adopted children.

"You consider that theory is persuasive?"

"I do when it turns out that Leroy photographed Brad Mitchell and Dr. Wagner together, albeit simply chatting together, and it later turns out that they were, in fact, having an affair, and she went on to become the director of his multimillion dollar clinic in White Plains."

Dehan leaned forward with her elbows on her knees. "Sir, there were five people in that house when those kids were killed. The logic is irresistible: either a sixth person was there and the Mitchells are protecting them, which makes practically no sense at all, or a sixth person arrived unnoticed and killed them, which is so difficult as to be virtually impossible, or one or both of the Mitchells killed those kids. There is no other possible explanation."

He went into a kind of dark sulk and muttered, "Dear Lord!" Then he scowled at me like it was my fault people did that kind of thing. "Impossible for a sixth person to arrive? Are you sure? Why?"

"Yes sir, because they would be seen either by neighbors or by the Mitchells. We have been over it from every angle. The blackmail angle is just about all we have, and the only thing that makes logical sense. It has to be explored and, hopefully, eliminated." I paused, thinking, and added, "Though that will leave us with only very bizarre options indeed."

He sighed. "I'll see what I can do, but let me warn you it is going to be very hard to find a judge sympathetic to what you want to do."

Dehan shrugged. "Then maybe you can get them to explain to us who the sixth man was, and how he got in."

She earned herself a rare scowl, he gave us the order, and we left. We took Dehan's Toyota and made the ten-minute drive down Soundview and Lacombe to the Mitchells' house on Turneur Avenue. As we were arriving, Dehan said to me, "They won't be there, and the nurse is going to insist on calling the Drs. Mitchell."

I shrugged. "That's okay. She'll have to call them after we go in. Her option is that we call for backup and knock the door down. She won't want to do that."

We pulled up outside the white house, with its decorative

white railings, and Dehan killed the engine and looked at me. "This kid is not going to talk to us."

"Maybe. I'm not convinced. My gut tells me something inside him is desperate to tell somebody what he saw. But neither his mother nor his father wants to hear him, either because they are being overprotective, or because his silence suits them."

She put her hand on the door handle and stopped.

"His father is a psychiatrist. He knows the kid needs to get this out of his system."

My face told her I agreed. "Sure, so what is it that's stopping him from doing what his son needs?" I shrugged. "Go figure."

We climbed out of the small car and made our way through the white, wrought iron gate and up the stone steps to the front door. We rang, and after a moment the door was opened by a young woman in a modern nurse's uniform. She was tall and angular, with thick black hair that wasn't so much curly as matted. She had a severe face and a green overall, and on her feet she had clogs.

She said, "Yes?" as though it were an advance rebuttal of anything we might have to say.

We showed her our badges. "I am Detective John Stone of the New York Police Department." I thought I had better spell it out for her. "This is Detective Carmen Dehan. We have a court order . . ." I extracted it from my pocket and showed it to her. "It requires Marcus Mitchell's parents and/or guardians to grant us access to him, to attempt to speak to him."

She took the order and read it, shaking her head. "I cannot do this. It's impossible. Not without Dr. Mitchell's consent."

"On the contrary." It was Dehan, picking the order out of the nurse's hands with her fingers. "You can and must. This is an order of the court, and it applies to you, with or without Dr. Mitchell's consent. Otherwise, in ten minutes' time, you will have this place crawling with cops carrying battering rams. Now, I suggest you show us the way to Marcus' room, and then you telephone whichever Dr. Mitchell it is you need to get consent from."

I smiled and pushed past her. Dehan followed and closed the door. The nurse just stood and stared at us.

I offered her what you might call a thin smile. "What's your name?"

"Thelma."

"Well, Thelma, you had better show me the way to Marcus' room, or I will prosecute you for contempt of court and obstructing a homicide investigation. Snap out of it, nurse."

She gave a small gasp and hurried across the broad living room toward the stairs. We followed her stumping clogs up to a wide landing, which we crossed to a white door. Here she paused and stared at us. There was a kind of horror in her eyes.

"He has not spoken for six years. He is deeply traumatized. He does not move or react or respond. Please, be gentle with him. What he saw . . ." She shook her head, closed her eyes, and opened the door.

The room was bright. Double windows stood open onto the rear lawn, and lace curtains wafted gently in the cold breeze. Angles of light lay across a bright patchwork quilt composed of luminous orange, red, and yellow squares. The room was large, broad, and spacious. There was an armchair in a far corner, a pine chest of drawers, and a freestanding oak wardrobe.

Marcus was lying in the bed. I had always imagined him as a child, but he was now about seventeen. He would have been a handsome young man, with a sensitive, intelligent face, had he not been so thin and drawn. The quilt was pulled up to his chest. His hair was platinum, his skin very white, and his eyes very blue. He didn't look at us. He seemed to gaze in the direction of the wardrobe, but without seeing it.

Dehan turned to the nurse.

"Thelma, we will be very gentle with Marcus. There is no need for you to worry or even to be here. In fact, you had better go and telephone the Doctors Mitchell. They'll want to be here." She paused a moment then continued and asked the question I had been turning over in my own mind. "Thelma, before you go, when you said you could not let us see Marcus without Dr. Mitchell's consent, which doctor were you referring to, Brad or Emma?"

Nurse Thelma lifted her chin. "Dr. Emma Mitchell. She is the mama, the one who cares for her boy. Dr. Brad Mitchell has nothing to do with him."

Dehan nodded. "Yeah, that's what I figured. Okay, you can run along now, and call the doctors."

The nurse left, and Dehan closed the door. Under the window there was a straight-backed chair. I went, pulled it over beside the bed, and sat. Dehan dragged over the armchair on the other side and placed herself close beside him, directly in his line of vision.

I said, "Hello, Marcus, my name is John, and that lady over there is Carmen. We are police officers, and we have some news for you."

I paused a moment to allow those facts to sink in. I noticed Dehan looking at me curiously.

"We are here to find out who killed your sister, Lea."

It was almost imperceptible, but there was a hardening of his face, like all the muscles had contracted at the same time. I had been wondering how long it had been since anybody had spoken to him about his sister. I figured it had been a long time, years maybe, and what I'd said had been a shock. I went on.

"It has been a long time now, hasn't it? Six years, but it's a crime that just won't go away, right? It's always down there, in the shed, with your sister, and Lee, and you. Alone."

I waited. I counted fifteen slow seconds in my mind and saw the smallest flicker in his eyes as he focused on Dehan. She smiled.

"You were alone," I said. "The three of you. It's important that there are no mistakes. You were alone. And then there was somebody there, and Lea was screaming. Lea was screaming a lot." I saw the bright reflection of tears in his eyes and felt a hot jolt of excitement in my gut. I said, quietly, "And you can remember how you felt in that moment."

The tears spilled down his cheeks. Dehan glanced at me. His bottom lip curled in, and his face creased up. He made an agonizing, guttural sound, and Dehan was on her feet. She knelt by his side, holding his hand and stroking his face. His eyes found hers and held them as he wept. She whispered to him, "What happened, Marcus? What happened?"

He screwed up his eyes and sobbed. Dehan stroked his hair, and he clung to her arm, curling up against the pain in his gut and in his heart. I rose and walked around to the far side of the bed, hunkered down beside him and Dehan. She gave me a look that said, *Don't talk.*

Slowly his sobs settled down, and I spoke again.

"Marcus, I know how much this is hurting you. I know it hurts you every day, and you don't want to talk, and you don't want to hear. But I also know that somewhere deep inside you, you *need* to talk. You *need* somebody to hear about all the pain you felt when you saw what happened to Lea. I know that you *need* somebody to share and understand what you are feeling."

He was still clinging hard to Dehan's arm, and again the tears spilled from his eyes as he squeezed them tight.

"That's why Carmen and I are here. We have come to hear your story, Marcus."

Now his sobs were convulsive, but silent. A couple of times they subsided but then welled up again, and he curled on his belly, like there was a vacuum there, of pain, that was sucking him in.

After about five minutes his breathing slowed, and he opened his eyes. He still had a hold of Dehan's arm. His sight drifted from an empty place in space to focus on Dehan's eyes, and then on me.

"John . . ." It was barely a whisper. I smiled at him, and his face creased into something like an expression, an echo of a smile remembered from six years before.

"Dad," he said, and the smile faded from his face. "Dad is coming."

Dehan frowned, shot me a look, and looked back at Marcus. She stroked his hair and asked, "Your dad is coming?"

His eyes were starting to glaze, and the lids were drooping. "Dad," he said again. "Dad is coming." And his eyes closed him into sleep.

We sat like that for a while, Dehan and I staring at each other, thinking in silence. Outside the room we heard the tramp of feet coming up the stairs. The door opened, and Brad Mitchell stepped in. He stared for a long moment at his son, who was still clinging to Dehan's arm. He stared at her a moment and then stared at me.

His voice was a rasp. "What the hell do you think you are doing?"

I stood. "Our jobs, Dr. Mitchell. Maybe it's time you started thinking about doing yours."

His face flushed with anger. "Why, you . . . ! How dare you . . . !"

"I'm not talking about your job at the university, Dr. Mitchell. I'm talking about your job here, at home, with your son, as his father. He still calls you dad. Did you know that?"

"What? He spoke . . . ? What the hell has been going on here?"

I crossed the room so that I was standing barely a couple of inches from him. "He just told us, 'Dad is coming.'"

His eyes went wide. "He said that?"

"He's been six years in this state, and it took me all of five minutes to get him talking. First he started weeping. Then he clung to Dehan's arm and smiled at us. After that he spoke. He said, 'Dad is coming.'" He swallowed hard, and I pressed a finger against his chest. "Maybe it's time you stopped being Dr. Mitchell for a while and started being Dad. He needs to talk, and he needs to talk to a friend, or a father, not to a damned doctor!"

He shook his head. "You're insane."

"Why?"

"Because of my wife, goddamn it! She will never allow it!"

THIRTEEN

WE LEFT NURSE THELMA WITH MARCUS AND WENT down to the living room. He gestured us toward the sofa and chairs and went to the sideboard to pour himself a generous whiskey, neat. When he'd taken a pull, Dehan asked him, "What is it about your being a 'dad' for Marcus that your wife would object to?"

He gave her a curious look, approached the chair beside the sofa where Dehan had sat, and lowered himself into it.

"After Lee and Lea were murdered, and Marcus was diagnosed with catatonic depression, naturally I set about finding the best people to treat him and help him come to terms, in as much as any person can come to terms with such a thing, with what had happened, with his traumatic experience." He paused and took another swig. "Naturally, as you'd expect, all those therapists agreed on one point, that he needed to address—*and deal with*—what had happened in the shed; but more to the point, more *precisely*, it was not the event itself he had to deal with. It was the *memory* of what had happened, his *emotional response* to what had happened." He shook his head, as though dismissing any argument to the contrary. "It is not the event that lives on in Marcus. That would be absurd, a physical impossibility. It is his emotional response that lives on within his memory, and is poisoning his mind and his emotions. And it is the *memory* of the event which needs to be dissolved, and dealt with. And for that he needs to replay the memory and disassociate himself from it emotionally."

I said, "But your wife will not allow him to do that."

"No." He took another swig and shook his head. "She says it is out of the question. And when we have tried, she goes completely hysterical, threatens to divorce me and take Marcus with her . . . More trauma for the boy, more suffering, more unhappiness. For the last five and a half years she would not even allow me to visit the boy in his room unless she was there. If I want to see him, I have to sneak home while she's at work."

"Where is your wife now? I would have expected her to be here."

"She's teaching a seminar and has probably given strict orders that she is not to be disturbed. Otherwise I assure you she would have been here before me."

I reached in my pocket, pulled out the court order, and handed it to him. He read it carefully and nodded. "Good." He placed it on the table beside his chair. "Good, maybe this way the boy will get the treatment he needs." He paused a moment. Then he frowned at me. "You say he spoke . . . That is extraordinary."

I recounted what had happened. About halfway through he began to smile. When I had finished, he asked me, "Have you studied any psychology, Detective?"

I shook my head. "Not really. I have read a fair bit of Freud, Watson, and Skinner." I smiled. "The other Mitchell, the English one."

"Juliet, she's a very fine psychoanalyst. One of the few women who truly understand Freud." He paused, nodding at the floor. "Your instinct led you very surely to what poor Marcus needed."

"It was common sense, Dr. Mitchell, nothing more . . ."

"You are quite right, but common sense is something that somehow seems to dissipate in rarified, academic environments."

He buried his face in his hands, and his voice became muffled. "That is what I need: to dispense with all the *bullshit* and get real again, remember who I was before I became Dr. Brad Mitchell. It is so easy to lose one's way. Common sense, yes. A lot of it is common sense."

Dehan spoke up. "Something inside him wanted to vomit out the memory, just like your stomach wants to vomit out food that is off, or too much tequila or whiskey."

He laughed. "Psychic reflux?"

I smiled. "Something like that. I'm not a psychiatrist, but Detective Dehan and I both saw clearly that he needed to talk." I gestured at the paper on the table beside him. "That court order places no limit on how often or how many times we can talk to him. I mean to give him time to rest, and then talk to him again, and again, until we find out what happened that day. Do you plan to obstruct us?"

He threw back his head and laughed out loud. "Obstruct you? I could not be more grateful to you, Detectives! This has been a living nightmare for me for the last five years, since Emma effectively robbed me of my son, my last remaining child. I love her dearly, but she can be excessively controlling. Now, there is some hope that I might get my boy back." He paused, tilted his head on one side, and gave a small, eloquent shake. "But you must know that my wife will be a very different story."

"Yes." I nodded. "I am aware of that."

"She will fight tooth and nail to stop you."

Dehan cleared her throat. "Dr. Mitchell, there are a couple of questions I would like to ask you. Marcus could not possibly have known that you were arriving when you did. So, what do you think he meant by, 'Dad is coming'?"

He took a deep breath and held it. "Off the top of my head I'd say that he was perhaps reliving that day, that terrible thing had happened, and he could hear me calling to them, and running toward the shed."

She nodded. "The other thing . . ." She hesitated a moment,

gathering her thoughts. "You're an eminent psychiatrist, your wife is a doctor of sociology. I believe that sociology requires at least a basic understanding of psychology, and having lived with you for . . . how long?"

"Twenty-five years."

"Having lived with you for twenty-five years, as a highly intelligent woman, she must know, beyond a shadow of a doubt, that Marcus *needs* to face what happened and deal with it."

He was nodding. "And your question is, why is she so deeply opposed to it?"

"Yes. If she was hysterical, or stupid, even uneducated, I could understand it. But she is a university professor who must have a good understanding of psychology . . ." She shrugged. "It makes no sense to me at all."

He gave a small snort of a laugh. "If you're thinking that she is trying to conceal evidence, you're wrong, plain and simple. It's nothing that exotic. Parents—not just women, men will do it as well—can get intense, hormonal reactions when their children are in danger. Hormonal imbalances can turn intelligent people into raging morons, idiots, and savages . . ."

"Killers?"

He looked her in the eye. "Oh, for sure. It sounds absurd, but a surge in certain hormones can bring out the very darkest in the human soul."

I studied his face a moment, wondering if he was trying to tell us anything. I decided I wasn't sure and said, "I have a final question for you, Dr. Mitchell. Where were you last night between eight and midnight?"

"Why, I was at home."

"Can anyone vouch for that?"

He frowned. "You're asking me for an alibi? Why do I need an alibi for last night?"

Dehan said, "Can you answer the question please, Dr. Mitchell?"

"I was at home with Emma."

I sighed. "Can anyone besides your wife vouch for that?"

"No." He thought about it for a moment. "No, we were alone. The nurse had gone. But why? Why are you asking me this?"

I studied his face carefully as I spoke. "Sonia Laplant, Lee's aunt, was murdered last night."

His face went tight, contracted, and he stared at me, then at Dehan, and back at me again. "*Sonia?* Why? That's insane! And you think that *I* . . . ? Why on Earth would I want to kill poor Sonia, for God's sake?"

Dehan shrugged. "For that matter, why would anyone want to kill Lee, or Lea? Logical explanations are something this case is pretty short on, Dr. Mitchell."

He kept staring at her, like she'd said something outrageous. I asked him, "Did you and Sonia stay in touch after you adopted Lee?"

He turned to me. "In touch? No. Why would we?"

"So you had no contact with her at all after Lee moved in?"

"No, I mean, minimal. We had sporadic contact, but nothing you could call staying in touch. When Lee pulled his attempted blackmail prank, she spoke with Emma, but aside from that, no, nothing to speak of."

Outside, the sound of a car pulling into the drive made us look. It was a silver Mercedes. Brad Mitchell got to his feet and spoke absently, staring out of the window.

"Emma . . ."

We heard feet running, the key in the lock, and then the other Dr. Mitchell burst into the room. She stopped dead, with the door open, staring from me to Dehan, and then her husband. Her voice, when she spoke, was shrill with anger.

"What the hell is going on?"

Brad Mitchell picked up the piece of paper and held it out to her. "They have a court order, dear."

She stared at it, like it was an insult. "A court order . . . ?" She shifted her eyes to meet mine. "I'll have your job. I'll ruin you. I'll destroy you. Have you . . . ?" She turned to her husband. "Have they hurt him? Have they been in? Did you stop them?"

I stood. "Get a grip, Dr. Mitchell. I'm going to ignore the stupid things you're saying because you're upset. But I am going to need you to get a grip."

Her face flushed red. "A *grip*? Are you trying to patronize me? Is this some macho sexist shit? The NYPD sending its big bully to intimidate a helpless woman?"

Dehan was on her feet. She came over beside me and looked down at Emma Mitchell.

"Why don't you talk to me, Dr. Mitchell? Why don't you threaten me with the loss of my career? You going to destroy me too? You going to accuse me of being a big, macho bully?"

Emma Mitchell's mouth worked, but no sound came out.

"Quit griping and do something for your son, for a change. Yes, we were upstairs in his room. Yes, we talked to him, and yes, within just a few minutes he spoke to us. Six years you've had the poor kid stewing in his own damned nightmares, and today, for the first time, he was able to get some of that crap off his chest. You don't want to hear it, but that's tough shit, Doc, because you're going to hear it. He hugged me, and he smiled at Detective Stone, and then he spoke to us. And you know what that smile said to me? It said he was grateful. Because what *you* have been doing for the last six years is to keep that poor little bastard locked in hell, and Detective Stone just gave him the key to get out."

They stared at each other in silence, then Emma Mitchell spoke in a dangerous whisper.

"Get out of my house, and don't *ever* set foot in here again."

I took the court order from Brad Mitchell's fingers and handed it over to his wife.

"This is a court order requiring you to give us access to Marcus Mitchell, so that we can speak with him. If you defy this order, you will be in contempt of court and liable to a prison sentence."

I paused to examine her expression. I figured she wasn't

listening to a damn word I was saying. She was just staring at me like she wanted to tear out my heart and eat it. I sighed.

"We are conducting a multiple homicide investigation, Dr. Mitchell. If you try to obstruct us, I will prosecute you to the full extent of the law. You had better pipe down before you go too far. We will give Marcus every care and help we can, but we will talk to him."

"Get out."

I nodded. "Okay, we'll go. But we will come back, and we will continue talking to him."

She pointed a trembling hand at the door.

"*Out!*"

I glanced at Brad Mitchell, but he avoided my eye. I gave Dehan the nod, and we left, stepping out into the cold, bright morning. We walked to Dehan's Toyota. She opened the driver's door, and I turned, leaned my back on the car, looking at the broad living-room window where I was in full view, and pulled my cell from my pocket.

The chief answered after a couple of rings.

"John, how's it going? All good?"

"The Mitchells weren't in when we arrived. The nurse allowed us to see the kid, and we managed to get him to say a few words."

"Oh, you did? That is extraordinary."

"Yeah, nothing very enlightening. He just said, 'Dad is coming.' He got very emotional and cried a lot, but he also smiled at us and hugged Dehan's arm. I'm not sure what it all means yet, but we both had the feeling he was really grateful for the opportunity to talk. After that he went to sleep. Then Brad Mitchell turned up, we spoke to him, and he was very cooperative. He welcomes the chance of therapy for the kid."

There was a frown in the chief's voice. "Then why doesn't he provide it? He's a psychiatrist, for crying out loud!"

"The problem is the wife, sir. She is opposed to it and has just thrown us out of the house. She says she plans to get me fired and to destroy me. She is going to cause problems. Sir, we need the Mitchell house watched, and if she tries to remove the kid, we need her to be arrested."

He was silent for a moment, then said, "Yes, very well."

"And, sir, I'd like to make it obvious. Let's have a patrol car sitting outside the front gate. I want to send her a clear message. She can't threaten and browbeat the police department."

"All right, John. That's fair enough. I'll send Sanchez and Olvera. They'll be there in ten minutes."

"Thank you, sir."

I hung up. Dehan was leaning with her forearms on the door, smiling at me.

"You're a nice guy, Stone. You have a lot of heart and compassion. I like that in you. But you are also a real son of a bitch. And I say that with the greatest admiration."

I smiled at her, then stared back at the big windows. I could see Emma Mitchell staring back at me.

"I am not motivated so much by wanting to bring Emma Mitchell down a peg or two, though I do want to do that. I am more concerned with the kid, Marcus. I worry for him." I turned to look at Dehan. "Is she trying to protect him, however misguided? Or is she trying to silence him? She's a dangerous woman, Dehan. How far will she go to get what she wants?"

The smile faded from her face, and she followed my gaze to look at the window.

"Jesus, I had never seriously considered her as a suspect, Stone."

"I wonder if Brad has. She is very intense, and he is scared of her."

She nodded. "I noticed that. He obeys her."

I sighed. "What the hell did that poor kid witness? What happened that day, Dehan? Who went down to the shed?"

"They both claim they both did . . ."

I grunted. "But logic dictates that whoever went down killed the kids."

She screwed up her face. "So, if it was one or both of the Mitchells, why didn't they kill Marcus?"

A prowler turned into the road, cruised up to us, and parked in front of the Corolla. The doors opened, and Sanchez, five foot four of solid muscle, and Olvera, six foot two of solid muscle, climbed out and joined us.

"Detectives."

"Good morning, Sanchez, Olvera, we need some surveillance on this place." I pointed openly at the house, knowing that Emma Mitchell was watching me. "Our primary objective is to prevent them from removing a young man of about seventeen. He is in a catatonic state, and we are trying to get protection from the court. He also happens to be our only witness in the homicide of two kids."

Olvera nodded. "The Mitchell case."

"Correct. So, if they try to remove the kid, you stop them. Arrest the mother if you have to."

"You got it, Detective."

"But one other thing, this is also a display of force. So there is no need to keep it low-key. This woman has threatened us with destruction and the loss of our jobs if we carry out an order of the court, so let's show her just how worried we are."

Sanchez grinned. "Sure thing, Detectives."

We thanked them and left.

FOURTEEN

Headed north on Castle Hill, Dehan asked me, "How worried are we?"

"Very."

She gave me a curious glance. "Why? What has you worried suddenly?"

I screwed up my face, trying to squeeze some coherent thought out of my brain. "I think I have been looking at this all wrong."

"Suddenly you're thinking that Emma Mitchell is the guy."

"What would her motive be?"

She made a face, glanced in her mirrors, and came to a halt at the lights on the Bruckner Boulevard.

"I don't think she's got one, Stone. Aside from anything else, look how damn protective she is of her son. I can't see a woman like that hurting her daughter."

"Nyah..." I said, like I meant it.

"Nyah? What the hell does *nyah* mean?"

"She *is* hurting her son, Dehan. She's one of those women who smother-mother."

"Smother-mother. That's great."

"Yes, one of those women who overprotect, and end up

causing more harm to the kid than what they are trying to protect the kid from . . ."

She gave me a bland look. "Ain't it sad when bad things happen to good sentences? That said, for some reason I understand you. But even so, those women hurt their kids by overprotecting them, not by sticking knives in them. I just don't see Emma Mitchell hurting her own daughter, whatever the case about Lee. Your phone is ringing."

I pulled my cell from my pocket. The screen said it was Joe, from the lab.

"Joe, what have you got."

"John, if you're free, you need to come and see this."

I glanced at Dehan. "Head for the lab. We'll collect the car later." To Joe I said, "We're on our way, what is it?"

"I don't know what this woman was into, John, but there are photographs stored in a password-protected file that you need to see."

"Okay, we'll be there in ten minutes."

I gently shook my head for a while as we sped east and north toward the Jacobi. Eventually I said to myself, "This is like a spaghetti junction of the mind."

She looked at me curiously. "I think that's the first time I ever heard you admit that you were confused."

I grunted. "Don't get used to it." And after a moment I wagged my finger. "Points that we can nail down."

"Not many of those."

"No," I said, a little sullenly, as we turned into Seminole Avenue past the oddly named Albert Einstein College of Medicine. Every time I went by I wondered if it was for people who were relatively ill. I didn't share that thought with Dehan. Instead I said, "Marcus witnessed the murder of his sister, Lea, and his adoptive brother, Lee."

She nodded. "Solid fact."

"Emma Mitchell does not want Marcus to talk to us, or anybody else, for that matter."

"Also a solid fact, but possibly a misleading one."

"We are not interpreting right now, Dehan. We are just stating facts."

She pulled into the hospital parking lot and parked the Toyota in the shade of a big plane tree. As the engine died, she said, "Lea's throat was cut, Leroy was stabbed in the back, while Brad Mitchell was running to the shed. Fact."

"And the only people in the house were the Mitchells and their three children. Fact."

She spread her hands wide and shrugged. "Of the two Doctors Mitchell, only one, Brad Mitchell, has anything approaching a motive."

I nodded just once. "That we know of. But while Brad Mitchell has been nothing but helpful and cooperative, Emma Mitchell has been nothing but obstructive." I paused a moment, then added, "Fact."

She sighed noisily through her nose and climbed out of the car. I followed.

We made our way to the lab and found Joe in the small cubicle he called his office. He was sitting at his desk with a manila file open in front of him. Inside the file was a small stack of glossy eight-by-ten photographs. He looked up as we came in and smiled.

"Hey, the dynamic duo. How's it hanging?"

"Could be better, could be worse. What have you got?"

He arched his eyebrows and shook his head. "I don't know. This was a file on her computer, called BM and MW. It was password protected. Pretty basic security. When we got in, this was what we found."

We sat, and he slipped the file across the desk to us. There were eight pictures. Each one of them was of Dr. Brad Mitchell and Dr. Margaret Wagner. They were not at the university. They were outside what appeared to be a small, country hotel. In the first they were pulling a couple of cases out of the trunk of a car. In the next the car had gone, and they were standing, holding each other in a deep kiss. In the third one they had emerged from the kiss, and she was holding his face tenderly, while he had his arms around her waist. In the fourth they were climbing the steps to the hotel entrance, arm in arm.

The next four showed them walking on the beach, holding each other and also kissing. I looked up at Joe. He said, "I'm still printing. There are another twelve of them. Twenty altogether. There are five taken with a telescopic lens through the hotel window which are definitely X-rated."

He turned the screen of his computer so we could see them and clicked through them one by one. When he came to the hotel window, Dehan wolf whistled. He had not exaggerated.

I sank back in my chair. My brain felt as though it was stretching like an overinflated balloon. "So, she was blackmailing him." I looked at Dehan. "Sonia was blackmailing Brad Mitchell. So much for her concern that Lee was taking after his father instead of his mother."

"Not only that, but she was actually using Leroy as her go-between."

I shook my head, like I was trying to clear it. "But, what does that make Brad? The most cunning, devious, evil genius on the planet? How can he play it so cool and come across as so sincere?"

She nodded. "I agree. He was totally credible." She turned to Joe. "We confronted him with the fact that the kid had tried to blackmail him. He not only admitted it. He told us that when the kid showed him a photograph of him with this woman, he laughed and called his wife to come and see the picture. She confirmed it."

Joe smiled. "That's one cool customer."

"Too cool," I said. "I find it hard to buy it. He must have known that the first photograph was a shot across the bows. They must have warned him that there were more, and more incriminating. It makes no sense that he would call his wife, show her the photograph, and tell her what the boy had done."

Joe frowned at me. "But that *is* what he did. There is no would or wouldn't about it. He did it."

I studied him a moment, and Dehan studied me. I heard myself say, "Unless somebody is lying."

Joe and Dehan looked at each other like I was nuts. Dehan said, "How do you figure that?"

"I don't know." I stood, but there wasn't enough room to pace, so I just made a couple of ineffectual turns with my hands on my hips. I drew breath to speak, but Dehan said, "Only two people could be lying. Assume Brad killed the kids, that would mean Emma is lying about them having breakfast, hearing the screams, and Brad running out ahead of her to the shed. According to her, remember, she arrived just a few seconds later. So that begs the question, why would she lie to protect her daughter's killer? Even if it is her husband, surely murdering her daughter would be enough to overcome her loyalty to him."

I grunted. "I know."

"So assume Emma killed the kids, for some motive we do not yet know about. That means Brad is lying about having found the kids, because he is trying to protect his wife. The same question applies. This woman just killed his daughter. What possible reason could he have for protecting her—*especially* as we now know he was having an affair with Dr. Wagner."

"I know, I know!"

"So that leaves the third option."

Joe said, "That they both did it."

Dehan nodded at him. "Exactly, that they both did it. Again, for some motive we do not know about yet. And I have to say I find it so improbable as to be fantastic, that those two would conspire together to kill their own daughter, or to protect their daughter's killer."

"And yet," I said, "one of those scenarios has to be at least partly right. Simply because there is no other possible explanation."

Dehan and I stared at each other for a long moment, and Joe stared from Dehan to me and back again. Then I said, "Unless . . ."

Joe said, "Unless what?"

"Unless Lea was not intentionally killed." Dehan frowned and drew breath, but I silenced her. "Wait! Just hear me out for a moment. Maybe we are getting stuck in a rut here. We are assuming that the only person with a motive is Brad. Because he was being blackmailed by Lee and Sonia. But how do things change if, just for the sake of a thought experiment, we assume that the Mitchells have an open marriage? Let's assume that Brad was not phased by Lee's threat because he knew that his wife would not mind. Maybe she knew about it already and approved, because she's having an affair or two herself."

Dehan made a face. "She did come on to you a bit when we first spoke to her."

Joe snorted a short laugh. "You old dawg, you."

I ignored them both and kept going. "So he happily calls in his wife, and they both laugh it off and hope that by doing that they have killed off the blackmail attempt. But like Brad said, he suspected there was somebody else behind it—Sonia. And Sonia knows that it ain't all that simple. Maybe Emma doesn't care if Brad is having an affair, but what about the university? What about the press? Let's not forget he is planning to open a multi-million dollar clinic. And what about the general public's impression of him, when he is trying to sell his services to people recovering from drug and alcohol abuse? If he is perceived as a libertine, or worse, a sexual predator who is exchanging positions of responsibility at his clinic for sexual favors, his clinic will be finished before it ever gets off the ground. Now *that* . . ."—I wagged a finger at both Dehan and Joe—"gives both Brad and Emma a very powerful, *financial* motive. Because she wants that clinic open as much as he does. Maybe she's even invested money in it. We need to look into that company."

Dehan shrugged. "Okay, but what about Lea?"

"I'm coming to that. So, Brad and Emma conspire to kill Lee, and they set up this elaborate story on which they both agree. But before they can execute it, something goes wrong."

"Like what?"

I tried again to do some pacing but found myself a couple of inches from a steep rack of shelves loaded with various types of paper. I turned my back on it and took a single step to the center of the room.

"There is an accident of some sort, and Lea is killed."

"No way, Stone." She stood and leaned against the doorjamb. "I know what you're driving at, and maybe it's the right direction, but it is pretty hard to accidentally cut your own throat."

"Or somebody else's, for that matter," put in Joe. "Though, conceivably, an unlucky fall could cause damage to the throat that could then be disguised with a cut of a rusty knife . . . But to do that to your own daughter is pretty intense."

"If," I butted in, "they wanted to throw suspicion away from themselves."

Dehan puffed out her cheeks and blew. "That is *a lot* of supposition. *A lot!*"

"We need to talk to Frank and have him go over his notes to see if her wounds were consistent with that possibility."

Dehan raised her hands. "Whoa, whoa, wait a minute, what exactly are we saying happened here?"

"We're not saying anything happened. We are speculating about what might have happened. Let me run through it. We have the Mitchells at breakfast on Sunday morning. We assume that Lee, under the direction of Sonia, has been attempting to blackmail Brad. Brad has told his wife, and both of them are worried about the damage that Lee and Sonia could do to the project for the clinic. Now, what happens next is pretty much what they have both told us, with small but important changes."

Dehan stepped forward and leaned her hands on the back of the chair where she'd been sitting. "They hear the screams?"

"Yes. That happens just as they said. But they are not Lea's screams, they are Marcus' screams. Brad runs into the garden, followed closely by Emma. I figure they both recognized the screams as their son's. Brad is the first to arrive at the shed, and he finds Lea lying on the floor, with her throat badly damaged from having fallen onto, say, for argument's sake, a garden rake. It might have been a hoe, a spade, a wheelbarrow, anything with a metal edge. Try to imagine how he would react. His daughter is lying there dying, choking to death, and Lee, the kid who has been threatening to blackmail him and destroy his future, is right there, watching, perhaps bent over her..."

Dehan spoke almost dreamily. "He freaks. Rage and frustration overwhelm him. He goes crazy. He grabs the knife and plunges it into Leroy's back, just as Emma is walking in. There is a moment or two of hysteria, and then they both realize they are going to have to call the cops and explain what happened. I don't know which one of them decides, my money is on her; either way, one of them decides they have to make it look like Lea was killed by the same person who killed Lee. Otherwise, suspicion will fall on them. So they must alibi each other, and they must cut Lea's throat. Marcus witnesses all this and goes into shock, which becomes chronic catatonic depression."

Joe gave his head a sideways twitch. "That is heavy."

Dehan narrowed her eyes at me. "But we are still left with the question, why the hell is Brad so willing to cooperate? Why is he willing to give us access to the kid, while Emma is so violently opposed? If they are coconspirators, they should be at one, but they're not."

"Because he is a very subtle psychologist with many years of experience, and he knows that if he opposes us, we'll go after him, whereas if he cooperates, behind the scenes he can pull strings, call in favors, and even manipulate Marcus if he decides to talk."

Dehan dropped into the chair again. "So let me get this straight. We are now saying that Brad is the guy. We are saying that he killed Leroy and then Sonia Laplant, and that Lea was killed by accident."

Joe turned to watch me. I thought about it for a few long seconds and finally shook my head and said, "I don't know."

FIFTEEN

We walked through the cold, dappled sunlight, under the whispering trees, toward where Dehan had left the car. I had my cell to my ear, and after a couple of rings Frank, the ME, answered.

"I'm busy, what do you want?"

"Aside from your babies?"

"You can have them. I'll even pay you to come and take them away. While you're at it, take my wife and her mother too. Again, what do you want?"

"You remember the Mitchell case..."

"Yeah, hard to forget, especially in light of the Sonia Laplant murder."

"Right." We had arrived at the car, and I leaned against the trunk. Dehan leaned next to me. I put the phone on speaker. "So here's what I am wondering: the girl, Lea, if she had been running, tripped and fell, and hit her throat on something hard, like the edge of a wheelbarrow, or a hoe or a rake, could that have been disguised as a knife wound by cutting her throat with the same knife that was used to stab Lee?"

He was quiet for so long I wondered whether he had walked away from the phone.

"Frank?"

"Yeah, I'm thinking. It's pretty far-fetched, but stranger things have happened. Yeah, possible, it's certainly possible, sure. Why not? The cut would have to be rough, brutal, and bruising. A razor or a scalpel would not do . . ."

"But the knife in that case was a rusty gardening knife."

"Yes, I remember. The answer is yes, that kind of cut, administered very soon after the accident, could certainly conceal the original wound. Is that what you think happened?"

"I'm not sure yet, Frank. I'm just exploring ideas right now. Thanks."

I hung up. Dehan opened the car.

"We need to pull them in."

She climbed in, and I got in beside her. She spoke as she fastened her belt.

"Brad in one room, Emma in the other, and we take turns good-copping and bad-copping them. Make 'em think the other is selling them down the river. 'Brad says it was your idea to kill Leroy,' 'Emma says she came into the shed and saw you stab Leroy.' Sooner or later one of them is going to crack."

As we pulled out onto Morris Park, I drummed a rapid tattoo on the vinyl dash and said, "What about Dr. Margaret Wagner?"

"What about her?"

"What's her involvement in all this?"

She frowned at me. "Does she have to be involved?"

"I'm not sure. It seems to me that she and Brad have had plenty of opportunity to have sex."

She glanced at me again with a curious smile. "Crude . . ."

"Yeah, that's what I mean. If their relationship was just sex, they have had plenty of opportunity. She's single; we are assuming, at least to some degree, an open marriage . . ."

"What are you getting at, Stone?"

"Well, you saw the photographs. They looked like a couple. They went away together on a holiday or a break. They posed as a couple, in the same car, walking on the beach . . ." I trailed off.

"I've never had an extramarital affair, but as far as I know they usually involve sneaking in and out of motels while nobody is looking. But what Brad Mitchell and Margaret Wagner have seems to be more of a relationship than an affair. I mean, how long has it been going on? Several years."

"I don't know what you're driving at."

"Well, how likely is it that he would receive this threat of blackmail—a threat which affected her directly—and not tell her about it?"

"It's not likely, at all."

"So, I mean, I am just playing with ideas here, Dehan, but what if she was the sixth person at the house?"

"Jesus, Stone!"

"We have to consider that possibility, that all three of them were involved, like in *The Orient Express*."

"So, what the hell . . . ?"

I sighed, feeling like the blind guy who was leading the blind.

"Okay, here's what we do. Take me to Broadway, to collect my car. Then you go pick up Brad Mitchell. Get Sanchez and Olvera to pick up Emma. Don't let Brad and Emma talk to each other. I'm going to go get Dr. Wagner. We'll interview the three of them at the same time."

She didn't reply for a while, then said, "What if they refuse to cooperate? Or they lawyer up? We haven't got enough to arrest anyone."

"Then we know we're onto something." I sighed again, feeling restless, like I was missing something. "One thing is really clear to me, Dehan. The blackmail and the murders are intrinsic to each other. But . . ." I gently beat my brow with the heel of my hand. "I am also aware that I am not seeing something. Something fundamental. I am overlooking something obvious. It is right there, staring us in the face . . . But I'll be damned if I can nail down what it is."

"I gotta tell you, Sensei. This time I think we are on the wrong track somehow. I know." She held up one hand. "I know, the pool of suspects is almost nonexistent, but I don't love any of them. They are all possible, but not a one of them goes ping."

She dropped me at the French Roast and headed off south down Broadway toward the Psychology Department. I climbed in the Jaguar and headed north toward the Alexander Hamilton Bridge, and White Plains.

The drive took me a little less than forty-five minutes, and at shortly after noon, I pulled up outside the clinic and walked into the cool, echoing vault of the reception. There was an attractive woman in her late thirties behind the reception desk, who watched me approach with a smile and an arched eyebrow. I showed her my badge, and she arched both of her eyebrows.

"Detective John Stone, I'm here to see Dr. Margaret Wagner."

"Do you have an appointment?"

"No, but it is important."

"Well, I'm afraid you're out of luck, Detective Stone. Dr. Wagner went out about an hour ago, and she hasn't returned."

"Can you tell me where she went?"

"No. I have no idea where she went. She received a private call, said she was going out and didn't know when she would be back."

I looked at the badge on her right breast and read it. I spoke quietly but persistently.

"Mrs. Sykes, we are investigating a homicide in which two children were murdered. They were Dr. Brad Mitchell's children. Today, another homicide was committed in the same case, and one of the witnesses was murdered. I urgently need to talk to Dr. Wagner because, you see, she is also a witness in that case, and she might be at risk. So, I need the number of the person who called her. You don't have to give it to me, but it would be deeply irresponsible of you if you refused. Do you see that?"

She smiled at me with bedroom eyes. "You don't need to try that hard, Detective. I assure you, I am easy to persuade."

She checked the screen in front of her and scribbled a number on a piece of paper, then handed it to me. I thanked her and took the number outside to the car. Sitting behind the wheel, I checked

Brad Mitchell's number on my cell. It didn't match, so I checked Emma Mitchell's number. It did match. I called Dehan.

"Yeah, Stone."

"You got Brad but not Emma, am I right?"

"What are you, psychic? Sanchez said both Mitchells went out shortly after we left. Brad went to work, but Emma never turned up."

"No, she called Dr. Wagner a little over an hour ago and Wagner went out to meet her. She hasn't returned, and she told her receptionist she didn't know when she'd be back. Can you get a GPS fix on Wagner and Emma Mitchell's phones?"

"Yeah, what do you want me to do when I find them?"

"Depends where they are. If they're in the city, take a couple of cars and pick them up. If they're in White Plains, tell me and I'll go talk to them. Make it snappy, I'm on my way back."

"Okay, Boss."

She hung up, and I sat staring at the dash for a couple of minutes, then fired up the big growler and headed down the drive.

She called me back as I was approaching White Plains.

"Okay, we have Emma Mitchell at the farmers market at the intersection of Martine Avenue and Court Street. I can't be exactly precise, but she's either buying tomatoes in the street or she's in Macy's. Right now she doesn't seem to be moving."

"No sign of Wagner?"

"No, none."

"Okay, I'm on my way."

It was a five-minute drive. I parked on Mitchell Place—it seemed somehow appropriate—and walked a hundred and fifty yards to the heart of the market at the intersection. There were hundreds of people, perhaps a thousand or two. It was information overload. The stalls: red, green, blue, yellow; the clothes: every shade of color under the sun from beige to crimson, lemon yellow to blue, orange, and green; and faces and bodies, thousands of faces and bodies of every shape and description, all of them moving, jostling, walking, pushing, not a single one where it had been fifteen seconds earlier. I felt a sinking sensation in my gut. Where should I begin? How did you search a place that was constantly changing?

I moved slowly through the crowd while it flowed past me like a teeming river. I tried to scan the faces, the clothes, the hair, looking for something recognizable, somebody who might be Emma Mitchell. There was nothing. As I walked, I pulled my cell from my pocket and called Dehan.

"Hey."

"I'm at the market, walking north along Court Street. Where should I be looking?"

"Okay, you have Macy's ahead of you on your left, across Martine Avenue. She's either at a stall there, beside the store, or she's inside Macy's. I figure she's talking to somebody because she has hardly moved in the last fifteen minutes."

"Okay, I'll check the market stalls. Stay on the line and tell me if she moves."

I shouldered my way through the crowd and crossed the avenue. A vegetable stall, a bald guy in a suit and a trench coat. A woman in a pink-and-white wool hat buying tomatoes. A girl with piercings in her nose selling potatoes to a black woman in a fur hat. Both laughing. A fruit stall. A stack of bright orange oranges. A gay couple buying apples. A woman pointing at a pineapple. The guy selling it, big, with big hairy hands. A stall selling clothes. A blond woman inspecting a sweater. A cheese stall. A man in jeans and a Barbour tasting a slice. A black guy talking to him and pointing at the cheese. Kids running, chasing each other. A woman with a red bike. Faces. Hundreds of faces. And hundreds of milling bodies.

Dehan: "You went past her."

I stopped, turned, scanned every face in a fifty-foot radius.

"She's not here."

"Go inside then. She must be in Macy's."

I pushed through the crowd and through the glass doors into Macy's. The aisles were as packed as the streets had been outside. I stood and scanned each stream of humanity as bodies jostled by me.

"This is impossible."

"Stay with it, big guy, she's there. Keep moving north."

"North?"

I made a mental adjustment and started walking past perfume and makeup stands. I saw an escalator and rode it to the next floor. Through acres of plate glass I could see people milling around clothes racks, pausing, taking clothes and looking at them, feeling them, holding them up against their bodies, checking mirrors.

"You're practically on top of her. Where are you?"

"Clothing department."

"Dressing rooms."

"Hell…"

I moved past the racks, searching the crowds, wondering what the hell Emma Mitchell was doing at Macy's in White Plains shopping for clothes. It was bizarre. And why wasn't Wagner with her?

"Any sign of Dr. Wagner yet?"

"Nothing."

"Have you spoken to Brad Mitchell yet?"

"No. I was waiting for you."

"What the hell is she doing here, Dehan?"

"Ask her."

"I would if I could find her."

I came to the dressing rooms. There was a woman in her fifties folding clothes. A badge on her chest said her name was Lisa. I showed her my own badge and said, "I'm looking for a woman, late forties, blond, blue eyes, slim, attractive, her name is Dr. Mitchell. Is she in there?" I pointed at the changing rooms.

She looked at me with large, brown eyes and said, "I don't know."

"Would you mind looking for me? This is a murder inquiry,

and I need your help." I smiled at her and tried to mean it. She smiled back.

"Well, since you ask so nicely. What's it worth?"

I gave her twenty bucks, and she winked at me, then went inside and started calling, "Dr. Mitchell! Dr. Mitchell!" I heard a few curtains swish open and then closed again, with a few muttered, "Sorry, darlin'," and then she came back. "No Dr. Mitchells here, handsome. Maybe try the johns. They're over there."

"Thanks."

"You want help there too?"

I gave her another twenty and followed her through the store, listening to Dehan saying, "... blond, blue eyes, slim, *attractive* ... yes indeed. Blonde, blue eyes, slim ... *attractive* ..."

We came to a short passage. The men's toilet was on the right. On the left was the women's. She pushed through the door while I waited outside, and I heard her voice asking, "Is there a Dr. Mitchell here? Is there a Dr. Mitchell in the house?"

She was funny. There was a murmured response and some laughter. Then I heard knocking, and, "Dr. Mitchell?"

Silence. A moment later a couple of women came out, gave me a strange look, and walked past.

"Dr. Mitchell ... ?"

I went to the door and pushed it open. There was a small group of women gathered around the shop assistant, who was gently pushing open a cubicle door. They all stopped to look at me. I held up my badge. "NYPD. What's going on?"

Lisa looked at me. "There's a woman in there, but she ain't answering. These girls say she's been in there a few minutes now."

One of the girls spoke up. "She was in there when I come in, and she's still there now. She ain't talkin', answering, nor nothin'."

I went to the cubicle door and gave a firm push. Something heavy gave and slumped. I put my head around the door and saw Emma Mitchell sitting on the toilet, with her head leaning against the wall, staring at the door with bulging eyes and a slack mouth. At a glance I could see the four holes in her left breast, and the large bloodstain that had oozed from them. I could also see the powder burns on her dress.

I withdrew my head. "You ladies are going to have to stay here for a while. Dehan?" This last I said into the phone. "You'd better get yourself here ASAP." I moved to the door and stepped outside. "I found her. She's in a cubicle in the john. She's been shot in the chest four times. Put a BOLO out on Dr. Margaret Wagner. I'm going to hang up and call the local PD. I'm going to need some backup."

I hung up and called the local PD, then went back into the toilet. The shop assistant was peering round the cubicle door. I growled at her, "Tampering with evidence is a felony, Lisa. Don't touch a thing. The woman in there has been murdered. The White Plains Police Department is on its way. Meanwhile, you can start by giving me your names and addresses."

They all stared at me blankly, and then all as one said, "*Murdered?*"

SIXTEEN

They had to take the door off the cubicle so they could pull her out and lay her on the tiled floor. She looked shocked, like the ceiling was the last thing she had expected to see above her that day. The Westchester medical examiner had come in from Valhalla and found that Dr. Emma Mitchell had been shot in the heart four times at point-blank range. The shots had been tightly grouped and had all but destroyed the heart. That was the prima facie cause of death, pending a thorough examination. He would send a copy of his final report to Frank and to me by email.

After some wrangling between the local chief and Inspector John Newman at the 43rd, the local PD handed the case over to me as part of my current, active investigation, in exchange for the promise that I would send them a full report once the case was closed. The local crime scene team moved in to dust and photograph, and a couple of uniforms stayed on to take statements from all the women who had been in the toilet when the body was discovered, before they were allowed to go home or continue shopping. The statements told me nothing I didn't know already.

Dehan arrived when I was examining the lock of the cubicle,

where the door was propped against the wall. I looked up as she approached.

"It's not broken, but Lisa told me the door was not locked when she pushed it open."

"Lisa?"

"The shop assistant I paid forty bucks to, to see if Emma was in here."

She went and stood looking in at the cubicle. "Is she tall and slim and attractive?"

"I wouldn't know. I have eyes only for you. So, they both came in here to freshen up. Emma went into the cubicle, there was nobody else in the toilet, so Margaret seized the opportunity, leaned in before Emma could lock the door, and pumped four rounds into her heart. Then left at the hurry up."

"Jesus, Stone. This is like trying to untie the Gordian Knot with woolen mittens over amputated fingers." She turned to face me and sighed. "She's behaving like somebody who is tying up loose ends. But what loose ends has Margaret Wagner got? Is *she* the one who was blackmailing Brad? Is that why he set her up in the clinic? As part of the payoff? Jeez, I tell you, Stone, I'm getting brain-ache."

I nodded. "Tying up loose ends is right. We need to go and talk to Brad. There's an outside chance he knows where she would go. If anybody can tell us about her, it's him."

"But hang on a minute, Stone, am I alone in wanting to know what possible motive she could have for wanting to kill Sonia? Emma I get, at a stretch, though why she would want to kill her now, after all these years, precisely when the police have started looking at the case again, beats me. But at least there is the age-old motive of jealousy. But Sonia? Why?"

"No, you're not alone, Dehan. It's just that we have no one to ask right now. Let's go ask Brad. Until we find Margaret Wagner, he's the only person who might know."

She stared around the toilet for a moment, like somebody she could ask might appear on one of the walls. Then she sighed again.

"Yeah, I guess."

"Ride with me. We'll collect your car tomorrow."

Dehan talked, and I listened all the way back to the Bronx. By the time we got there and walked into the station house, things were about as clear as they had been when we'd left Macy's in White Plains. We had Brad taken up to interview room two and went to get some coffee.

When we entered the room five minutes later, he stood up. His face was flushed, and his eyes were bright with anger. Dehan placed a cup of coffee in front of him. He ignored it.

"What the *hell* do you think you're playing at? I *demand* to see my lawyer! If I am not under arrest, you *cannot* keep me here! I have cooperated with you in every way possible, but I have been here over *three hours*!"

We sat and watched him in silence until he sat down. When he'd done that, he said, "I am waiting, Detectives. And I should warn you I am not without influence in this town."

"Dr. Mitchell." I paused. "There is no easy way to say this. Your wife was murdered today."

At first he frowned, squinting, like we were stupid and he didn't understand what we were saying. Then his skin turned gray as the reality of it set in.

"Emma? What are you talking about? How . . . ? I mean . . ." He looked from me to Dehan and back again. "I don't believe you. Are you sure? Where is she? I want to see her."

"Yes, we're sure, Dr. Mitchell. That's why you've been kept waiting so long. We wanted to talk to you both, but when we went to get your wife, she was not at home or at work."

He was still incredulous. "Where was she? What happened?"

"We're not sure. We're hoping you can help us explain it. She was at White Plains."

"*White Plains?* What the hell was she doing there?"

"She called Dr Wagner. Dr Wagner left the clinic to go and

meet her, saying she didn't know when she'd be back. It looks as though they met in White Plains."

"She met with Margaret? What for?"

Dehan answered. "We don't know, Dr. Mitchell. That's what we are trying to tell you. Can you think of any reason why your wife would call Dr. Wagner and arrange to meet her there?"

His frown was growing deeper. "Well, why don't you ask her? What does Margaret say?"

"Margaret has disappeared."

"*What?*" Neither of us answered. There was a heavy silence in the room. He said, "What are you telling me?"

I leaned forward, holding his eye. "Dr. Mitchell, is there anything you need to tell us about Dr. Wagner? Anything you feel we ought to know?"

"No! *No!* Why? Just tell me what's happened!"

"We found your wife at Macy's, in the ladies' toilets, in a cubicle. She had been shot four times in the heart with a .22. We're waiting on ballistics, but it seems to be the same weapon that was used to kill Sonia."

"Dear god, sweet Jesus . . ."

He sank back in his chair. After a moment he covered his face with his hands and began to sob. Slowly he curled forward until his head was on the tabletop, making a painful keening sound. Dehan stood and left the room. I waited, watching him, wondering if any person could put on such a convincing act, or if what I was seeing was for real.

The door opened, and Dehan came back in with a cup of water and a box of tissues, which she placed in front of Mitchell. She put her hand on his shoulder and spoke softly.

"We can do this later, Dr. Mitchell, but we really urgently need to know where Dr. Wagner is."

He looked up at her, and his face was wet and shiny. "You can't think that she . . ."

"We don't think anything, Dr. Mitchell. But your wife has been murdered, and Dr. Wagner has disappeared. We don't know what's happened, but it stands to reason, doesn't it, that if she didn't kill your wife, she might well be another victim of the killer. So either way, we need to find her."

He swallowed and nodded. "Yes." He nodded some more. "Yes, of course. It's just so hard to take in. And poor Marcus... What am I going to do?"

"You could start," I said, "by telling us the true nature of your relationship with Dr. Wagner."

He stared at me with a slack mouth for a long moment, then took some tissues and blew his nose and wiped his eyes.

"When I married Emma, we both agreed that there were likely to be other people over the years. True fidelity is hard to come by, and when you find it, often enough it is false. So when Emma has had affairs, I have ignored it, and when I have had affairs, she has turned a blind eye. We agreed that we wanted each other as partners, as a family, but we also acknowledged that sexually we both needed variety. It worked for us."

Dehan frowned. "But Dr. Wagner was something more than that."

He sighed. "Yes, Margaret was somewhat more than that. The problem with Margaret was that I fell in love with her, and she fell in love with me, but then . . ." He held my eye a moment and then turned to Dehan. "Then Emma became infatuated with Margaret too, and Margaret enjoyed all the attention and the flattery, and she and Emma ended up having a brief affair."

Dehan sat. "Wow, way to keep things simple."

"Keep it in the family," he said, with a hint of bitterness. "In the end the affair with Emma ran its course, but my relationship with Margaret never quite ended. We have a lot in common, we genuinely enjoy each other's company." He sighed. "Anyway, that's why we found it so funny when Lee tried to blackmail me."

I grunted. "But the repercussions for you professionally, and for the clinic you were planning, could have been severe if the nature of your relationship with Dr. Wagner had been revealed."

"Yes." He blew his nose and took a second tissue to wipe his eyes and dry his cheeks. "That's true, and it did worry me some. But I have always been with the Duke of Wellington on that score, publish and be damned. I have nothing to be ashamed of, and frankly I think it's time society grew up a little."

"Did your wife and Dr. Wagner see it that way?"

"Emma did, certainly. It is also true that we were both wealthy in our own right. But Margaret had fought her way to eminence from near poverty. She had a lot to lose, particularly as regards the clinic."

Dehan said, "If backing for the clinic had failed, or if it had been shunned by the celebrities it was aimed at, it would have hit her hard."

"Yes." He nodded.

"So you decided to pay Sonia off."

He didn't answer. He stared down at the tabletop. Finally I told him, "We found the photographs."

He seemed not to hear but started talking.

"After Lea was killed, after Lee was killed, she revealed the full extent of what she had on us. We got together, Emma, Margaret, and I, and we discussed it, and we decided that the best thing to do was to make Sonia an offer, but make her understand that as far as Emma and I were concerned, we didn't give a damn if she published the pictures or not. We were doing it to protect Margaret, but we were only prepared to go so far in order to help her. It seemed to work, because for six years we hardly heard from her."

He paused, shaking his head. I said, "But a few weeks ago she tried to hike the price, and you said no."

"Yes, how did you know that?"

"It made sense. That's why she came to me with such an innocuous picture. It made little sense that Lee would try to blackmail you with a picture like that. But once she gave it that spin, that it was the blackmail that provoked the murder, we had to look into it. Then, when I saw the pictures she had on her laptop, it made me wonder why she had picked the least damning of all the pictures she had, to show me. That only made sense if she was putting a shot across your bows. A warning. Go with the price rise or face the consequences."

He drew a shuddering breath. "Yes, that was about the size of it. We were paying her monthly, but when she heard that the clinic was going ahead, she decided she wanted an increase."

Dehan gave a small grunt. "So Dr. Wagner, who had the most to lose in all this, took it upon herself to go to Sonia and shoot her dead."

"I find that very hard to believe. Margaret is a strong woman, but she is also kind and humane."

I scratched my chin, feeling vaguely uncomfortable. "Did you know, Dr. Mitchell, that Dr. Wagner had a gun?"

"Yes." He gave a small nod, still staring at the tabletop. "I bought it for her. New York is a dangerous city, and our business, though it may seem absurd, attracts some pretty dangerous customers. I mean that there are a lot of crazy people in this city, and many of them come to us for help. It's not unusual for a patient to become obsessive about a therapist."

Something made me ask, "Dr. Wagner is not from New York?"

"No, she's from South Dakota." He smiled wistfully. "She's your classic farm girl. Grew up on a ranch on the plains, not far from the Missouri River."

There was a moment's silence. "So, what gun did you buy her, Dr. Mitchell?"

He gave a small laugh. "Of course, she grew up with guns, and her father had taught her to shoot a pistol by the time she was twelve. She was partial to revolvers, so I bought her a single action Colt, a .45. I don't know much about guns, but it seemed to me to be a hell of a gun for a woman. However, she insisted that was what she was accustomed to. 'If you're going to stop somebody,' she used to say, 'you have to stop 'em dead.'" His breath shuddered. "In retrospect, perhaps I should have paid more attention."

"So she was a good shot."

"Very." He frowned. "She is a very good shot."

"Do you own a gun, Dr. Mitchell?"

"Yes, why?"

"What caliber is it?"

"Nothing like Margaret's. It's just a .22 revolver. I doubt I would have any accuracy with anything bigger, and frankly I don't want to kill anybody. If I have the gun, it is just to discourage, or perhaps wound, in extremis."

I glanced at Dehan. She was staring fixedly at him. I asked, "When was the last time you saw that weapon, Dr. Mitchell?"

He went very still. "I don't know. I keep it locked in a drawer in my consulting room at home. Weeks, perhaps a month. I detest guns."

Dehan spoke. "We are going to need to see that pistol. Sonia and your wife were not killed with a .45, Dr Mitchell. They were both killed with a .22."

His face flushed. "I did not kill my wife! I love my wife! I have not killed anybody!"

I nodded. "Let's not get ahead of ourselves, Dr. Mitchell. Nobody is accusing you of murder. We just need to go and get the gun, and let the lab boys run some ballistics tests on the slugs."

He half stood. "Look, let me go with you. I have to see my son. You have had me here for hours. He must be very anxious. Please! Let me go home and see my son. I have not hurt anybody. For God's sake! I wouldn't even know how to!"

I stood. "Take it easy. We'll all go to your place. We'll check on Marcus, and you can give us the weapon. Just answer me one more question before we go. Where is Dr. Wagner? Where would she go if she was on the run?"

He stared at me for a long time. "I don't know. I really don't know. I have no idea."

SEVENTEEN

We put out a BOLO in South Dakota generally, but we contacted the Blunt PD and the Hughes County Sheriff's Office asking them to be on the lookout for Dr. Margaret Wagner, probably driving a Mercedes S-Class sedan. Her parents had a ranch on Rocky Road, 206B, about twelve miles northwest out of Blunt. The sheriff told us he'd drop by and talk to them, to see if they had any idea where their daughter was, or might be. I didn't hold out much hope. Something told me a South Dakota rancher wasn't all that likely to sell his daughter out to a New York cop.

We got to the Mitchells' house, and Brad Mitchell led us to the room he had at the back of the house where he saw private clients. It was spacious, elegantly furnished in dark wood and leather, and had a consulting area with an old-fashioned couch and an open fireplace. But directly as you came through the door, there was an old oak desk with a big, black leather chair behind it. Dr. Mitchell headed straight for the desk, sat, and unlocked the top right drawer. From it he pulled out a steel case and unlocked that. He opened it and sat staring.

"It's empty." He looked up at Dehan. "Why?"

"When was the last time Dr. Wagner was here?"

He shook his head, thinking. "Six months? Maybe more. We

tended to meet at the university. Sometimes we went to her apartment on the Upper East Side. But she gave that up when she went to White Plains. She has her own apartment in the clinic. The last time she was here must have been six or seven months ago."

"Have you seen the pistol since the last time she was here?"

"Yes, of course. I told you. I clean it regularly. I must have cleaned it three or four weeks ago..."

I interrupted. "Who else knows you have it?"

He mouthed at me like a goldfish for a few seconds, then said, "Well, just Emma. Nobody else. Marcus of course, but he..."

Dehan cut in. "So, assuming Dr. Wagner has the gun, how did she get it? Has the lock been forced?"

She moved around the desk and hunkered down to inspect it. She looked at me. "Nothing."

I leaned on the desk and held his eye. "Did you give her the gun and tell her to go and kill Sonia?"

He was shaking his head, but I already knew he hadn't.

"Good grief, no! Of course not!"

"We've requested your financials, Dr. Mitchell. And we'll be examining Sonia's financials too." I lowered myself into a chair, and Dehan stood behind him, leaning against the window frame. "You've already admitted that Sonia was demanding more money, so what were you going to do? You told her no, and she threatened to make her photographs public. I figure she was going to send them to the university, maybe even the press, and investors in the clinic. What were you going to do? Try to weather the storm?"

"We talked about it..."

Dehan cut in. "Who? Who is 'we'?"

"I discussed it with Margaret at the clinic, and I discussed it with Emma here, at home. We hadn't really decided what to do. Emma said she and Sonia had always got on well, so she suggested she might go and talk to her. But I don't think that ever came to anything."

Dehan asked, "What about Dr. Wagner? What did she have to say?"

He gave a small shrug and a small shake of the head to go with it. "She said she'd leave it to me."

She glanced at me, and I knew what she was thinking. I sighed and stood. "Dr. Mitchell, I am going to take you in as a material witness. I'm also going to put a twenty-four-hour guard on the house because I am just not clear on what's happening here. I don't know if you and Marcus are at risk or not. But what is clear is that the witnesses to Lee and Sonia's blackmail scam are going down like flies. And that includes Lee and Sonia."

I called the chief.

"John, nice to hear from you. What can I do for you and Carmen?"

"I need the twenty-four-hour guard on Marcus Mitchell to be extended till we close this case. And I need a car to come and take Dr. Brad Mitchell in as a material witness in Dr. Emma Mitchell and Sonia Laplant's murders."

"I see. Anything else?"

I told him there was nothing else, and he hung up. Then I called Joe.

"John, how's it going?"

"Yeah, okay, listen, have you got the ballistics on the Emma Mitchell murder yet?"

"They came through about ten minutes ago."

"Can you compare them with the slugs recovered from Sonia Laplant? Something tells me it was the same gun."

"Hold on, John . . ." I heard him moving around and rattling keys. Mitchell was frowning hard at me. After a minute or so he said, "Yeah, you're not wrong. It was the same gun."

"Thanks, Joe." I hung up, looked at Dehan and then at Mitchell. "The same gun that was used to kill Sonia was used to kill your wife. I'm going to ask you one more time, Dr. Mitchell. Where is Margaret? Where would she go if she was on the run?"

"I don't know. All I can think is that she might try to go back home, to her parents' ranch. Other than that . . ." He shrugged and shook his head in a helpless gesture. "I have no idea."

I looked at Dehan and sighed. "South Dakota."

"One thousand, five or six hundred miles. Twenty-four hours, nonstop."

Outside we heard a patrol car roll up.

"Dr. Mitchell, I'm going to have to ask you for your keys. They'll be returned to you when you are released."

He stood and reached in his pocket, handed over the keys, and started to sob. His legs failed him, and he sank back into his chair, repeating softly, "Oh god, oh god, this can't be real, oh god . . ."

The doorbell rang, and Dehan went to answer it. Mitchell was staring at me with a slack mouth and a wet face. I drew breath to say something but realized there was nothing I could say. His whole world had fallen to pieces, and there was not a damned thing anybody could do to fix it.

Sanchez and Olvera came in. Olvera said, "Ogden and Santos are relieving us. We'll take Dr. Mitchell in."

I nodded. "Okay, Dr. Mitchell is a material witness to murder. He has just lost his wife. Look after him."

"Sure."

They helped him to his feet and took him out to the car. I stood at the living-room window, where Emma Mitchell had stood that morning watching me, and watched them help Brad Mitchell into the car, then I watched the car take off toward Lacombe Avenue. Dehan stood by my side.

"Stone, have you even the faintest idea of what the hell is going on?"

"Yes."

"You want to enlighten me? You were as lost as I was an hour ago."

I didn't answer at first. My eyes were fixed on the road where the patrol car had been moments before. I spoke absently.

"The person who shot Sonia was a bad shot. She missed her target with practically every shot, even though she was standing at point-blank range. But Emma was shot by somebody experienced in the use of firearms. The gun was held close to the target, and every shot found its mark even though the body must have moved and slumped during the shooting. The shots were fired fast, and without hesitation."

"The way daddy's little cowgirl might do it?"

"Yeah."

"So who killed Sonia?"

"Emma."

"Why?"

"To protect her son and her home." I turned to look at her. "The three of them were adamant they were not going to pay more, but Sonia, seeing the clinic opening, and Dr. Wagner appointed as director, must have realized they were not giving her anywhere close to what she could be getting from them. She was not about to let up, and when she came to me with this supposedly new evidence, Emma must have panicked. When she saw that we were not going to be put off, we were not going to stop digging, and that her husband was apparently not worried, she decided she had to take things into her own hands and put a stop to it."

"So she took her husband's gun and used it to kill Sonia. But what about Wagner?" She frowned and shook her head. "I don't get it."

I sighed. "Brad Mitchell was keen to help Marcus recover and start talking again. Emma did not want that to happen. I suspect Emma had begun to see everybody as an enemy and was planning to kill Sonia *and* Wagner, and frame her husband for it. If she pulled it off, all the witnesses to what happened that day in the shed would be either dead, discredited, or silenced, along with her husband's affair with Wagner. We'll probably never know, but that's how I figure it."

"Holy cow, Stone. Does that mean . . ." She faltered. "Are you saying you think Emma Mitchell killed her own daughter?"

"No, I think Lea was killed like we said, playing with Lee and Marcus, by accident. I think Emma was the first to arrive on the scene, not Brad, and in a fit of rage she killed Lee."

"Just as we thought happened with Brad, but it was Emma. And that's why she didn't want Marcus to talk. So who the hell killed Emma . . . ?"

I shrugged. "She pulled a gun on the wrong cowgirl. They'd known each other for years. Hell, they'd even been lovers. Maybe Emma lost her nerve. Wagner disarmed her, shoved her in the cubicle, and shot her without hesitation, the way she'd been taught since she was a kid. Then she ran."

We were silent for a moment, looking out at the front yard. "She's gone home."

I nodded. "I think you're right."

She frowned. "So, if you're right, Marcus is in no danger. What do you want the guard for?"

"In case I'm wrong. I won't be sure of anything until we talk to Marcus and Dr. Wagner."

She smiled at me, but it was a sad smile. "Road trip."

"Yeah, but we need to talk to the chief first."

By the time we'd made it back to the station house, it was well past lunch, and my stomach was reminding me of the fact. We found the chief in his office eating roast beef on rye with lots of salad. He dabbed his mouth with a linen napkin as we walked in and gestured to the chairs opposite.

"Please, sit, excuse me while I eat. Late lunch. I am trying to reduce the amount of red meat in my diet, you know. My wife makes me salad sandwiches, but then I buy roast beef at the corner deli and add it to the sandwich at lunch. A pointless exercise, I know, but . . ." He shrugged and smiled. "So tell me, progress?"

"Almost."

Dehan leaned forward, elbows on knees, and cut in.

"It's a bit of a mess, sir, but we are unraveling it. We now think the Mitchells have been colluding to conceal the fact that Emma Mitchell killed their adoptive son, Leroy."

"Good lord!"

"He and his aunt, Sonia Laplant, had been blackmailing the

Mitchells, and we suspect Emma Mitchell must have grown to resent the boy. On that Sunday morning when the murder occurred, we think it all started when Lea fell while playing and damaged her throat. By the time Emma reached the shed, the poor kid was already dead. When Emma Mitchell arrived on the scene, and saw Leroy over her dead daughter, she snapped, went into a rage, and killed Leroy by stabbing him with the gardening knife. Then, realizing they would have to call the cops, they decided to cut Lea's throat and make it look like some third party had broken into the backyard and killed the kids. It almost worked. It explains why Emma Mitchell was so opposed to getting therapy for Marcus. If he started talking, she would go down for the murder of Leroy, her adoptive son."

"Yes, I see. What about Sonia Laplant and Emma Mitchell?"

"We believe that recently, when Sonia saw that the Mitchells were opening a clinic in White Plains, pitched at the high end of the addiction market, she decided she was demanding too little in blackmail and tried to demand more. That's why she came to Stone with that photograph. It was a shot across the bows for the Mitchells, warning them she had more and more graphic pictures.

"When we started to investigate, especially when we got access to Marcus, Emma panicked and decided to take things into her own hands. She took her husband's pistol, a .22 revolver, and shot Sonia. She also decided to take out Dr. Wagner."

He frowned. "Why?"

Dehan hesitated, and I answered. "I think it was a combination of things, sir. The Mitchells had an open relationship where each turned a blind eye to the other's affairs. But Mitchell's relationship with Wagner had gone on for years, and from what I can gather, it may have been becoming closer. Coupled with Brad's lack of concern about Marcus talking to us, Emma may have been scared that she was about to be replaced. Mitchell and Wagner were going to get therapy for the boy, the boy was going to talk, and she'd go down for Lee's murder, leaving the way clear for Brad and Margaret to be together."

"Good heavens! This is, of course, all conjecture."

"It's highly educated guessing. It's also the only possible version of events that works. But as it stands, we can't take it to the DA. We need two things. We need Marcus to be made a ward of court until this is all over, and for him to receive proper therapy so we can find out what really happened that day."

"Yes, I think as things stand it would be hard for a judge to refuse."

"We also need to go to South Dakota."

"South Dakota? What in the world do you want to go there for?"

"Because, when Emma Mitchell tried to take out Margaret Wagner, in the Macy's ladies' toilets, in White Plains, we think Wagner disarmed her and shot her. And we are pretty certain she then panicked and fled back home to her parents' ranch."

"In South Dakota."

"Yes, and my gut tells me a cowboy rancher is not going to hand over his daughter to some New York cop without some pretty persuasive arguments, especially if he believes that his daughter was acting in self-defense."

"And you think you can persuade them?"

"Yes, sir, because I believe she was acting in self-defense."

He gave a small grunt. "You don't even know for sure that she's there."

"No, but we have BOLOs out just about everywhere, and this is our best bet. We should see it through."

He sighed heavily. "Very well. Go to South Dakota. But make it snappy and wrap this up before anybody else gets hurt. I'll talk to Judge Henderson about Marcus."

"Thank you, sir."

We made our way down the stairs and gathered our essentials from our desks. Dehan pulled on her jacket, and I climbed into my gabardine. At the door Dehan stopped and looked up at the cold, blue sky. A few clouds were gathering out over the Atlantic. She went up on her toes, bit her lower lip, and turned to me.

"Something's wrong."

"I know, I just don't know what it is."

"It all fits, it all works, but . . ." Her eyes flitted over my face. "It's Lea. Lea is wrong. I can't see why, but it doesn't work. That part of the story is wrong."

I sighed. "Yeah, you're right. Lea is wrong. Let's hope Marcus can tell us why."

"Yeah," she said, "let's hope so."

EIGHTEEN

Sonia and Mitchell's financials came through that evening just before I set about roasting a leg of lamb, and Dehan sat at the table and went through them. I had made two very dry martinis, punched holes in the leg and stuffed them with garlic butter, brushed the leg with olive oil and lemon juice, and covered it with fresh rosemary and Maldon salt, when Dehan leaned back and appealed to somebody called Jeez.

"Jeez!" she said. "This is enough to make you miss working with a real pro!"

I arched an eyebrow at her. "I beg your pardon, Carmen?"

"Not you, dummy. Sonia and Mitchell. Hell, Sonia looked smart, and Mitchell is supposed to be part of the intellectual elite of this country! Every month, for as far back as these records go . . ." She leafed through them. "Twelve months. Every month, on the first of the month, Brad Mitchell makes a payment of one thousand dollars. And every month, on the second of the month, sometimes the third, a thousand bucks shows up in Sonia's checking account. I mean, come on!"

I smiled and started peeling potatoes. "People don't realize the skill that goes into being a good criminal."

"You ain't kidding, big guy. Now, a month ago, five weeks, the payments stop. Two gets you twenty there is an exchange of emails, or more likely telephone calls, in which Sonia demands more money, and he tells her to take a hike."

"No doubt in my mind. Joe should confirm that for us in the next day or two."

She got to her feet and stretched, then took her glass and walked to the kitchen door. She opened it and allowed the cold night air to creep in. With one hand on the doorframe, she stood and looked out to the backyard. I knew she was seeing the Mitchells' backyard and the shed at the end beside the wall of trees. I put the potatoes on to blanch them and slipped the lamb into the oven at 400 degrees Fahrenheit. As I closed the oven, Dehan spoke absently, like her mind was somewhere else.

"So all that's left is to find Wagner and make her understand if she talks to the DA and claims self-defense there may not even be a prosecution . . ." She turned and looked at me. "And see if we can get Marcus to talk."

I took my martini over to her and kissed her nose. I do stupid things like that sometimes when nobody can see me.

"That's about the size of it."

She was pensive for a while, with one hand on my chest.

"This is going to sound stupid"—she looked up into my face—"but I don't want it to be either of the Mitchells. I think the Mitchells were nice people, maybe even good people." She shrugged and smiled. "A bit French for my taste, all that stripped pine and free love, but basically on the side of the angels. You know what I mean by that?"

"Yes."

"Emma went crazy. Who wouldn't, when your daughter has had her throat cut, your son has gone catatonic, and your husband has spent the last six years falling in love with another woman?"

"Sure."

She gave her head a small shake. "But I don't want to believe that she was a bad woman. I don't want to believe that she was capable of murdering a child, however much of a pain in the ass he was."

"I know. We'll know more tomorrow."

And I kissed her again, but this time it wasn't on the nose.

―――――

WE ROSE at six the next morning, and after a shower and a breakfast of strong black coffee and rye, we headed off at eight a.m. It was a long, tedious, and uneventful drive along one and a half thousand miles of straight roads and flat horizons. We arrived in Blunt at eight thirty the following morning. There are about three hundred and sixty people in Blunt, there is no deputy sheriff and no police department in Blunt, and, as far as I could make out, there was only one restaurant, the Medicine Creek Bar and Grill, at the gas station. So we stopped there for breakfast and to splash some cold water on our faces before heading on up to the Wagner ranch.

We had phoned ahead to the sheriff of Hughes County, who was located thirty miles away, at Pierre. He told us that visiting the Wagner ranch was high on his to-do list, but if we wanted to mosey on up ourselves, we were welcome to do that. We also called the Pierre Police Department and spoke to Chief Jonathan Davies Jr. to inform him that we were making inquiries regarding a murder investigation in the Bronx, New York. He told us they'd received the BOLO and we should go right ahead, and if we needed anything, all we had to do was ask.

In Dehan's words, "They don't plan to be obstructive, but they sure as hell don't plan to help either, if they can avoid it."

We checked in at the Dakotas Motel, just outside Blunt, dumped our bags, and then followed the road for another mile, through endless acres of flat fields under a spotless blue sky, till we came to an intersection. There we turned right onto Route 83 and headed north for a couple of miles through the same vast, featureless landscape. There we came to a wide, dirt track on the right of the road. There was no gate. Just a wooden post with a wooden sign nailed to it that read "Wagner Ranch." The track ran straight through cornfields to a large, L-shaped building in cream with sloping green roofs.

We pulled onto the track and rolled and bumped our way for half a mile to a broad expanse of dirt outside the front of the farmhouse. As we pulled up, the front door of the house opened, and a tall, strongly built man in a blue gingham shirt stepped out to watch us. I put him in his midsixties. He had a shock of silver hair and a severe face that said he had little time for BS and none for those who peddled it.

We climbed out, and the car doors had a flat, empty echo when we slammed them shut. We walked toward the man, and I pulled my badge from my pocket and held it up for him to see it as I approached.

"Good morning! Detective John Stone, from the New York Police Department." I gestured at Dehan. "This is my partner, Detective Dehan. Are you Mr. Wagner?"

He blinked once, and his eyes shifted to Dehan, then back to me.

"I'm not real interested in who y'are, mister. You're on my land, and I ain't invited you. So y'all can git right back in your fancy car and get the hell outta here."

"Sure, that's no problem. We'll be moving right along. I just wondered if you'd had any news of your daughter, Margaret."

"I already told you once, mister. I ain't interested in why you're here. And I already told you to git off of my land. If I have to tell you a third time, you'll be talkin' to my shotgun and my dogs."

I didn't say anything for a moment. I just nodded. I turned and took two steps back toward the car. Dehan was watching me and frowning like she thought I was crazy. Then I stopped and looked back at the man.

"We've driven twenty-four hours to be here, because we do not believe your daughter is guilty of murder. We haven't taken the case to the DA yet. We want to talk to Margaret first. She killed a woman. Did she tell you?"

He took a deep breath and looked back at his front door, like he was thinking about going in to get his shotgun.

I pressed on, "If the DA gets the case as it stands, Margaret will become a fugitive from the law. But we believe she killed Dr. Mitchell in self-defense."

His eyes were a pale blue and hard as diamonds, but he didn't move or say anything. I took another step, but back toward him this time.

"We believe Dr. Wagner tried to kill her, and she protected herself."

"That's a right every man and every woman has."

Dehan said, "It's what we have a Constitution for, right?"

His cold eyes shifted to her, and for a moment I thought I saw a glimmer of humor. It wasn't reassuring.

"I wouldn't give you an ounce of horseshit for the Constitution, 'Tective Dehan. My rights and my liberties are my own, and I don't need no Constitution to give 'em to me. Neither do I need no judge in Washington to tell me what they are. You tellin' me Maggie killed a woman protectin' herself. She got a right to do that. So what the hell are you doin' here on my land?"

I took another step. "I didn't tell you that Maggie killed a woman trying to protect herself, Mr. Wagner. I told you *we thought* she killed that woman in self-defense. But that doesn't make a damn piece of difference if I can't prove it to the DA."

"You take one more step, son, and I'll blow your head clean off your shoulders."

"Fine, Mr. Wagner, you do that. But it won't make any difference, except that you will then be dealing with the FBI instead of the NYPD, and they will be out to make an example of you, to prove to the nation that gun-toting, NRA rednecks will not be allowed to ride roughshod over the law and go around shooting law enforcement officers."

"You better watch that tongue o' yours, boy."

"Right now all you have to contend with, Mr. Wagner, is a couple of cops working a low-key case who want to hear your daughter's story because they believe she shot a woman in self-defense. Send us away, or shoot us, and you will have the whole damned federal system grinding into gear to come and get you. Not to mention the anti-gun lobby making a national issue out of you and your daughter."

He stood watching us for a long moment, then reached back, opened his front door, and called inside, "Honey, bring me my rifle, will you?"

I sighed. "Mr. Wagner, that is not necessary. We are going to leave. But you need to give our message to Margaret. Right now, with the help of a good lawyer, she could walk away from this scot-free. But keep this up, refuse to cooperate with the authorities, and she could be facing very serious trouble."

"I don't take kindly to threats, son."

"Oh, for Christ's sake!" It was Dehan who had exploded out of her silence. "He is not threatening you, you great lunk! He is trying to help you! And what should be more important to you, he is trying to help your daughter! You want your daughter to spend the next fifteen years in a state penitentiary? Have you any idea the kind of life your daughter has grown used to in New York? She lives in luxury in an old manor house, respected as an eminent expert in her field! You know what it would do to her to spend ten or fifteen years among killers? Do you know what they would *do* to a woman like her inside? You better put your dick away, Yosemite Sam, and start thinking with your brain!"

The door opened behind him, and a woman stepped out. Her dress was a nondescript gray-blue, as was her hair and her complexion, and her general aura. The one thing that was remarkable and memorable about her was the double-barreled shotgun she had open over her arm. She didn't hand it to her husband. She just stood staring at us, while he looked quietly back at her.

"Give me the gun, honey."

She glanced at him briefly, then looked back at Dehan. "No."

"Give me the gun."

"No, Hank, I wanna hear what they have to say."

"They ain't got nothin' t'say, goddamn it! They're just tryin' to persuade us to hand over Maggie." He looked at me with murder in his eyes. "Well that ain't never gonna happen."

I shook my head. "You don't have to hand her over. You just need to listen to what we are telling you, and then give my card to Margaret. She can call me and talk to me whenever she likes. All I want is to hear her story." I held up both hands. "I am going to reach for my wallet and pull out a card. Don't shoot me."

They watched me pull out my wallet and extract a card from it. I walked the short distance between us and handed the card to Mrs. Wagner. "Please, ask her to call us."

She didn't say anything, but her eyes were eloquent. I gave Hank a brief look, and his eyes were eloquent too, though they said something different. I turned and walked back toward Dehan and the Jaguar. On the way I caught Dehan's eyes, and I saw her eyebrows rise, and she jutted her jaw back toward the ranch house. Then I heard a voice.

"Detective Stone. Please, wait."

I turned. Margaret Wagner was in the doorway. She held a revolver in her hand, hanging loose by her side. Her father was glaring at her.

"Get back inside, girl! Are you out of your mind?"

"No, Dad. I'm not going to hide." To me she said, "What is the law, Detective Stone? If Mom and Dad are prosecuted for aiding and abetting a fugitive . . ."

I didn't answer straightaway. I sighed, feeling suddenly weary, sick of this case.

"That's not what should be worrying you, Dr. Wagner. The DA is not keen to prosecute cases that will be unpopular, or a waste of public money. Loyal fathers who protect their daughters from unfair prosecutions are not the flavor of the month. Nor are DAs who prosecute legitimate self-defense cases. But yes, if you refuse to come with us, and your parents persist in refusing to give us access to you, we will need to call in backup from the Pierre PD. And then there will probably have to be a prosecution."

Hank Wagner roared, "Don't listen to him! This is your home! These bastards will not take my daughter!"

"I don't want to take your daughter, Mr. Wagner. I just want to talk to her!"

Margaret Wagner placed her hand on her father's shoulder.

"Dad, it's okay. I am not going to drag you into this affair. I've caused enough trouble as it is. It's time to face the music and come clean."

She handed her mother the revolver she held in her hand and crossed the dirt to where Dehan and I were standing. She held out her wrists to me.

I shook my head. "Do you plan to shoot or strangle either of us on the way to the motel?"

Her eyebrows drew together. "No . . ."

"Then we don't need to cuff you. All we want is to talk to you, Dr. Wagner."

She dropped her hands to her side. "Oh," she said simply, and sighed. "Let's go then."

NINETEEN

We had bought coffee at the gas station, and now we sat in our motel room, with the window open to the cold sunlight, and the distant, vague sounds of voices, dogs, birds, and tractors. Dehan sat on the bed, Margaret Wagner sat in a sage-green, vinyl armchair by the window, and I sat on a straight-backed hard chair in front of the TV. Dehan was the first to speak.

"What happened in White Plains, Dr. Wagner?"

She took a moment, gazing out of the window, then met Dehan's eye and said, "To be honest, I am not exactly sure." She took a very deep breath and let it out as a heavy sigh. "This is not easy to explain. It goes back a long way."

I said, "So start at the beginning. We're not going anywhere."

"It all started when Brad had this brilliant idea of adopting some kid he'd read about in the paper."

"Leroy Brown."

"Lee, his aunt insisted his name was Lee. Anyhow, Brad is a real dreamer and an idealist. He can also be a very selfish bastard. When he had this idea, he didn't stop to think how it was going to affect his kids or his wife or his family as a whole. It was his latest fancy, and we all had to go along with it. I told him, right from the start, this is going to be a disaster, and you are going to be picking up the pieces for the rest of your life. He wouldn't listen, and back then Emma did whatever Brad said. He was a bully too."

Dehan asked, "So Emma was okay with the adoption?"

"She said she was, but the truth is the only person who had any real enthusiasm for it was Brad, because the ones who were going to have to deal with it day to day were his wife and his kids."

"What about you?"

She sighed again. "Yeah, what about me?" She made a helpless gesture. "We had a complicated relationship. I was in love with Brad. I have always been in love with Brad. Emma and I got on well, there was never any real jealousy, but we were both in love with Brad, and somehow that formed a bond between us. In the end we became a kind of family, but I was always on the outside. Emma was the queen of the house, I was part of the harem."

I cleared my throat. "Had that started to change recently?"

She winced. "Kind of, but let me get to that, because there are other things you need to understand. When Lee moved in, it was absolutely no surprise to me that almost right away he started to cause problems."

"What kind of problems?"

"The first month or two he was quiet and sullen. He refused to play with Marcus and Lea, he refused to speak to anyone, and he barely ate. I warned them both that he was going to be a problem, but they insisted he just needed to adapt and find his own place in the family structure."

Dehan asked, "And did he?"

Wagner gave a humorless laugh. "Oh, he did! Boy did he! And then some. He became aggressive and foulmouthed. Poor Marcus was always frail and sensitive. Lee caught on to this very quickly, and he started bullying Marcus mercilessly. He would punch him, kick him, swear at him, steal his clothes and toys . . . He was a monster. And Brad and Emma, who did not believe in punishing, tried to deal with it by having meaningful dialogues and family conferences, where everyone was free to say what they felt."

She threw back her head and laughed. "Well at first Lee would use those gatherings to swear, insult Brad and Emma, hit Marcus, once he even pissed on the floor. But pretty soon he realized that if he played along and pretended to be 'growing' and 'learning to integrate,' Brad and Emma would get such an ego rush, and be so pleased with themselves, that he would become the blue-eyed boy, so to speak, and any complaints that Marcus and Lea made against him would put them out of favor with Brad and Emma."

"Shoot, that's smart."

"Cunning. Lee was not especially intelligent, but he was about as cunning as they come." She paused a moment to think. "Well, obviously, that was not a situation that could go on indefinitely. It was not sustainable, and it was Emma who began to give under the strain. He was vile to her. He was always making lewd suggestions, insinuating that she was having affairs at work, that when he was older he would become her lover . . . it went on and on, and in the end she began to crack.

"When he saw that, as far as she was concerned, his days were numbered, that was when he came up with the blackmail scheme."

"Wait." I raised my hand. "Hold on a moment. What do you mean exactly by, 'his days were numbered' as far as Emma was concerned?"

She put her hand to her mouth. "Oh, god no. I didn't mean that at all. No, I mean that he had lost her as an ally and she was beginning to think in terms of actually returning the child into foster care. Brad was dead against it, but the strain had started to get to Emma, and I know she was very unhappy, and so were the kids."

"And that was when Lee came up with the blackmail idea."

She nodded. "Initially it was just a way of ensuring they did not send him away. He had some idea that Brad and I were involved because, though we didn't advertise it, neither did we hide it. The five of us, me, Emma and Brad, and the kids, were very comfortable with each other, so it was not exactly a secret. Thing was, Lee was such an ignorant little brat that he *thought* he had detected an affair. So he threatened Brad with revealing that supposed affair to his wife. Brad laughed."

Dehan nodded. "He told us about that. He called his wife and showed her the photograph."

"Yeah, that wasn't a brilliant move, as it turned out. Lee was humiliated and furious. He told his aunt about it, and that sweet, lovely woman turned out to have a pretty deep, dark side. She saw the potentials that Lee was too young and too naïve to understand. We had mentioned to her, just chatting, that we had plans to set up a rehabilitation clinic in White Plains. It came up because she worked with Dr. Garrido at the rehabilitation center in the Bronx. It was an innocent comment that had far-reaching consequences. She realized that if our relationship was conducted quietly and discreetly, there would be no consequences, but that if it was brought to the attention of the university and the press, the consequences could be catastrophic. It would put an end to the clinic, to our careers, to everything.

"So she took it upon herself to spy on us, follow us, and photograph us. And then she went to Brad and Emma with her photographs and demanded payment for her silence. Brad, naturally, was all for what he called 'publish and be damned!,' but Emma and I persuaded him to think of the kids and of his family as a whole. In the end we decided to tell her we were prepared to pay a sum every month, equivalent to a salary, for her silence. She agreed, and for a short while we had relative peace. Even Lee seemed to settle down for a while.

"Then Lea and Lee were killed."

I raised my hand again. "Dr. Wagner, let me ask you, were you there that day? Were you at the breakfast table?"

"No, I was away in San Francisco, at a seminar, and I can prove it."

"But they confided in you as to what happened that day?"

"Yes, they telephoned me that evening and told me about it."

"What was it exactly that they told you?"

"That they had been reading the paper and drinking coffee

after breakfast, in the kitchen, they had heard screams, and rushed to the shed. There they had found Lea and Lee, dead."

Dehan cut in. "Did they say which one of them arrived first?"

She paused to think and frowned. "Now that you mention it, no. But I think they said Brad found them. I have always understood it that way. Anyhow, that was six years ago, and for the past six years we have paid Sonia faithfully every month. But, about six weeks ago, roughly, Sonia spoke to Brad and told him that she wanted her cut, as she put it, from the proceeds of the new clinic. Her cut was to be twenty-five percent of the profits, annually. He told her no, categorically. So she said she would send all the photographs she had to the university, and to the press. She also said she would tell the cops Lee had tried to blackmail them and that she suspected one of them had killed him. She said she would destroy the three of us."

I nodded. "So Emma killed her."

"Yes. How did you know?"

"It had to be either her or you. You would have used the .45 that Brad gave you, and you wouldn't have missed."

She gave a soft grunt. "That's for sure."

"So what happened in White Plains?"

"She had been in a state of anxiety ever since Sonia had threatened to send the photographs to the university, and to go to the cops. When you showed up and started asking questions, and especially when you decided you wanted to talk to Marcus, she started spiraling out of control. She and Brad had argued. He had told her several times he would take care of it, but she didn't believe him. Brad talks a good fight, but the fact is he's full of shit."

She sighed, seemed to gather her thoughts, and continued.

"She called me at the clinic. She seemed to be on the edge of hysteria. She said she needed to see me urgently. I told her to come to the clinic, but she said no. She didn't want to be seen. She wanted to meet at the entrance to Macy's." She gave a small laugh.

"I told her it was market day and the place would be full of people. She didn't care. That was where we had to meet.

"When I got there, she was jumpy and real nervous. She told me she had done something crazy. I asked her what, and she kind of bundled me into the corner of the door, got real close up to me, and said she'd killed Sonia."

She shook her head and looked away out of the window. She bit her lip and shook her head again. I could see that she was crying.

"I couldn't believe it. I had known her for years. I loved her. I would never have imagined her capable of doing something like that. She said she'd had to do it, to protect Marcus."

I said, absently, "To protect Marcus?"

"He needs constant care. If the clinic fails, it will be a financial catastrophe for all of us, but especially Marcus. He will have no one to care for him."

"So what did you do?"

"I told her she had to go to the cops, get a lawyer, plead temporary insanity. I would certify it. I remember when I said that she laughed. It was a weird laugh. It made my skin crawl. She said, 'I know you would, darling,' she hunched her shoulders, and ran her hands over her upper arms. It still makes me shudder. Then she said she was desperate to use the restroom, and would I go with her, then we'd have lunch and talk about what to do. I agreed. My idea was, while she was in the restroom, I would call Brad and the cops. But it didn't work out that way.

"When we got there, she started acting real crazy. There were a couple of women in there, and she chased them out, saying she needed the place to herself. And that was when she pulled the gun on me. It was a small revolver, .22 caliber. She was waving it around like a crazy woman, pointing it in my face, at my chest, repeating over and over that she'd killed Sonia and she'd have no problem killing me."

Dehan interrupted. "But what was her motive?"

"She said she knew that Brad and I were conspiring to get rid of her, and once she was gone, he and I would get married."

"How did she think you were going to get rid of her?"

"She didn't make a lot of sense, to tell you the truth. She was terrified that we would allow Marcus to start talking. I told her surely that would exonerate her and Brad and work against Sonia. But she was hysterical and convinced that we were going to manipulate Marcus and fill his head with false memories."

She stopped again, staring down at her hands in her lap.

"Anyhow, it became clear nobody was coming to my rescue. She pushed me violently toward one of the cubicles, and I knew she was going to kill me. I acted without thinking. I twisted the gun out of her hand, spun her round, and pulled the trigger, the way my daddy taught me. Before I knew it, she was dead, and I bolted. I came home, told Mom and Daddy what had happened, and tried to think what the hell to do." She heaved another big sigh. "I'm glad you showed up. I might have done something really stupid."

My mind was still lingering over something she had said. I dragged my mind back to it and frowned at her. "You still have the gun?"

"It's back at the ranch. All the prints are still on it, though Daddy tried to persuade me to wipe them off."

Dehan shook her head. "That's something we don't really need to know. It's enough that you tell us that for the last couple of days they have been trying to persuade you to hand yourself in."

She smiled. "Oh, yes, I guess so."

I said, "We'll have to take you back with us, Dr. Wagner, you realize that? We'll need the gun too, but I am going to recommend to the DA that they do not prosecute. But we will need your full testimony to close the case on the murder of Lea and Lee."

Her eyebrows rose, and her face said she was surprised.

"You are going to close that case?"

"Yes. Just as soon as we get back to New York."

We rose and made our way out to the car. Dr. Wagner climbed in the back of the Jaguar, and Dehan and I slung our bags in the trunk.

"So you are going to close the case? Were you going to tell me about it at some point, big guy?"

"I assumed you picked up on what she said."

"What she said?"

"Yeah, about Emma. All we need is to confirm it with Marcus, but I think it's pretty clear, don't you?"

She nodded a couple of times down at our baggage. "About Emma."

I smiled and said, "Exactly. Come on, let's get going."

TWENTY

Dr. Simone Robles was sitting beside Marcus, with the cool sunlight from the bedroom window slanting across her ebony face. She had a notepad on her knee, and she was watching me carefully. Marcus was on her left, propped up in his bed. He was also watching me. Dehan was sitting on a straight-backed chair on his left, holding his hand, and beside her was Dr. Wagner, in an armchair, watching Brad Mitchell across the other side of the bed, beside Simone Robles.

I was at the foot of the bed, in another armchair. I was watching Marcus. I smiled at him and saw the flicker of a response.

"Marcus, it's nice to see you again. You do not have to speak if you don't want to, but I think I have worked out what happened all those years ago, in the past, and all of these people here really need to know."

He blinked, and I saw a faint wash of color in his pale neck and cheeks. I smiled again.

"So I'll tell you what we are going to do. I am going to tell all these people what I think happened. And if you think I am wrong about anything, you let me know. You can either interrupt me and say, 'Come on, John! You're talking out the back of your neck, dumbo!'"

There was a small ripple of sniggers around the room, and I saw a twitch of a smile on Marcus' face.

"Or," I went on, "if you want to, you can tell me I'm right on the money. But if you prefer not to talk yet, you can just squeeze Detective Dehan's hand. Once is 'That is correct,' twice is 'That is wrong.' Okay?"

After a moment Dehan smiled at me and said, "That is correct."

Simone looked at Mitchell and raised her eyebrows. He looked at me, and I like to think there was a touch of awe in his expression. Who knows?

"So, you, Dr. Mitchell, and your wife were in the kitchen, as you told us, reading the Sunday papers. You had the kitchen door and windows open, and the kids were outside playing. At first, Detective Dehan and I had played with the idea that a sixth person had entered the house, either invited by one of you, or by Lee, and that that person had killed Lea and Lee. But when we examined the house, we realized that the only form of access was via the driveway, and that anyone arriving that way would risk being seen by you. Also, because the kids and the shed would be invisible to anyone approaching that way, it would make the crime one of opportunism. Which made no sense because the opportunity only became apparent *after* the person had entered the backyard. It made no sense.

"There was also the question of escape. The killer had had no opportunity to escape by the time you reached the shed. Emma had told us that when you heard the screams you went to the window. So you would have had to have seen him leave, but you didn't. And if he had left after that, you would have had to have intercepted him as you approached the shed. But when you got there, it was empty. So it became very clear to us that there was no sixth person. The murder had to have been carried out by one of you."

I took a deep breath, leaned back in the chair, and crossed my legs.

"But that presented us with another problem. Though blackmail provided some motive for killing Lee..."

"No, it never did!" It was Mitchell, shaking his head. "We never took that seriously."

Margaret Wagner interrupted him. "Oh, for god's sake, Brad, pull your head out of your ego from time to time. *You* were never worried by it. But Emma was worried sick by that threat, and so was I, if you must know. Everybody was sick to their back teeth of that brat except you, because you hardly ever had to speak to the little monster!"

I saw Simone Robles smile as she made notes and raised my hand.

"Excuse me. Save it for later, please. Allow me to continue. From a police perspective, Dr. Mitchell, blackmail provided a motive for killing Lee, but it did not explain Lea's killing. And whichever way we examined it, we came up with the same problems that the original investigating detectives found. There was no way of explaining Lea's murder."

I turned my eyes to Marcus. He was staring at me fixedly.

"Then it occurred to us that the explanation might be a simple one. That Lea's death might have been an accident. That while the kids were running around, she might have tripped and struck her neck on some object, like the side of a wheelbarrow, or a hoe. Then, I speculated, Emma Mitchell might have arrived first, before you, Dr. Mitchell, and seen Lee bending over her dead daughter. Already under intolerable stress from the boy's threats and behavior, and from seeing her family falling apart because of him, she took the knife and killed him. And then, to try to deflect the blame from herself, one of you cut Lea's throat, concealing the bruise and making it look as though an unknown killer had murdered both kids."

I heard Mitchell rasp, "No, no, never! We would never . . . !"

But my eyes were on Marcus, whose face was bright red, while his knuckles were white where he was gripping Dehan's hand.

"It was," I said, "the only viable theory we had. But there were aspects that troubled both Detective Dehan and me. Then it came to me, when Dr. Wagner was telling us about her meeting with Emma in White Plains.

"She said that Emma was terrified that you, Dr. Mitchell, and Dr. Wagner would, and I quote, '. . . allow Marcus to start talking.' She then added, 'I told her surely that would exonerate her and Brad . . . But,' Dr. Wagner said, 'she was hysterical and convinced that we were going to *manipulate Marcus* and fill his head with *false memories.*'"

I paused, sighed, and shook my head. "This woman, Emma Mitchell, was holding a gun on Dr. Wagner, accusing her of trying to frame her for the murder of Lee and Lea, so that she and Brad could be rid of her and get married. Emma's full intention by then was to kill Margaret Wagner; there was absolutely no reason for her to pretend she was innocent of the killing. Her very motive for killing Dr. Wagner was her *belief* that she was being framed. So clearly, if she believed she was being framed, she didn't do it."

There was a deathly silence in the room. Outside, in the backyard, a bird was chirping sporadically. I said, "So, if she didn't, who did? We were out of options. And then another thing struck me that should have struck me much earlier. It probably would have if we had not been looking at an apparently inexplicable situation. But in retrospect it was obvious.

"If Lea had fallen and struck her throat on a hoe or a wheelbarrow, she would not yet have been dead by the time you arrived. She would have been asphyxiating. But she showed no signs of asphyxia. There was, according to Dr. Mitchell's account, and the crime scene photographs, a huge amount of blood at the scene. Lea had bled out from her wound, which meant she was still alive when she received it.

"The only possible explanation was that Lea had her throat cut before you arrived, by Lee Brown. As happens with so many abused kids, he acted out what had been done to him on another, more vulnerable child. He was no stranger to violence and death —he had killed his own mother. My suspicion is that he was trying to rape Lea, as he and his sister had been raped by their father."

I caught the movement and looked over at Dehan. She nodded. "He says that is correct."

I nodded and smiled at him. "And you tried to rescue her, didn't you, Marcus?" He leaned his head against Dehan's arm and started to weep. I went on, "You tried to take the knife from him, but it was too late. He had already killed her. You had had enough, you had all had enough, he had destroyed your happy family, and now he had murdered your sister. Maybe you even feared for your own life. You took the knife from him and killed him. Is that right, Marcus?"

Dehan nodded and said, quietly, "That is correct."

Dr. Simone Robles gestured me to be quiet, stood, and hurried around to hunker down beside Dehan, talking quietly to Marcus. Mitchell had folded in on himself and had covered his face with his hands, sobbing like a child. After a moment Wagner went over and, in a strange echo of Simone Robles, she hunkered down in front of Mitchell, took one of his hands, and started murmuring softly to him.

I stood and went to the door. Looking back, I could see that Marcus was now clinging to Simone Robles and Dehan was getting softly to her feet. She joined me at the door, and we stepped out onto the landing, closing the door quietly behind us. Olvera and Sanchez were there, waiting.

"Give them a while, take their statements, no need to book anybody."

We moved down the stairs and out into the cold, bright light of the morning. Clouds were gathering in the east. Rain was coming, and with it the spring.

I turned to Dehan. "We need to brief the chief and the DA."
She nodded. "And then?"

"And then?" I unlocked the burgundy growler and leaned on the roof. "And then I need a good, rare sirloin at the French Roast, and a good bottle of fine red wine."

"But first ersters, please, and Gewurztraminer."

"Indeed, first ersters, Gewurztraminer, and then Argentine sirloin."

"And then Bushmills and that cheese that smells like rotting feet."

"Yes, and then that. And a taxi home."

We climbed into the big burgundy beast and drove away from the Mitchells' house, in Castle Hill.

Don't miss ALONG CAME A SPIDER The riveting sequel in the Dead Cold Mystery series.

Scan the QR code below to purchase ALONG CAME A SPIDER.

Or go to: righthouse.com/along-came-a-spider

NOTE: flip to the very end to read an exclusive sneak peak...

DON'T MISS ANYTHING!

If you want to stay up to date on all new releases in this series, with this author, or with any of our new deals, you can do so by joining our newsletters below.

In addition, you will immediately gain access to our entire *Right House VIP Library*, which includes many riveting Mystery and Thriller novels for your enjoyment!

righthouse.com/email

(Easy to unsubscribe. No spam. Ever.)

ALSO BY BLAKE BANNER

Up to date books can be found at:
www.righthouse.com/blake-banner

ROGUE THRILLERS
Gates of Hell (Book 1)
Hell's Fury (Book 2)

ALEX MASON THRILLERS
Odin (Book 1)
Ice Cold Spy (Book 2)
Mason's Law (Book 3)
Assets and Liabilities (Book 4)
Russian Roulette (Book 5)
Executive Order (Book 6)
Dead Man Talking (Book 7)
All The King's Men (Book 8)
Flashpoint (Book 9)
Brotherhood of the Goat (Book 10)
Dead Hot (Book 11)
Blood on Megiddo (Book 12)
Son of Hell (Book 13)

HARRY BAUER THRILLER SERIES
Dead of Night (Book 1)
Dying Breath (Book 2)
The Einstaat Brief (Book 3)
Quantum Kill (Book 4)
Immortal Hate (Book 5)
The Silent Blade (Book 6)
LA: Wild Justice (Book 7)

Breath of Hell (Book 8)
Invisible Evil (Book 9)
The Shadow of Ukupacha (Book 10)
Sweet Razor Cut (Book 11)
Blood of the Innocent (Book 12)
Blood on Balthazar (Book 13)
Simple Kill (Book 14)
Riding The Devil (Book 15)
The Unavenged (Book 16)
The Devil's Vengeance (Book 17)
Bloody Retribution (Book 18)
Rogue Kill (Book 19)
Blood for Blood (Book 20)

DEAD COLD MYSTERY SERIES
An Ace and a Pair (Book 1)
Two Bare Arms (Book 2)
Garden of the Damned (Book 3)
Let Us Prey (Book 4)
The Sins of the Father (Book 5)
Strange and Sinister Path (Book 6)
The Heart to Kill (Book 7)
Unnatural Murder (Book 8)
Fire from Heaven (Book 9)
To Kill Upon A Kiss (Book 10)
Murder Most Scottish (Book 11)
The Butcher of Whitechapel (Book 12)
Little Dead Riding Hood (Book 13)
Trick or Treat (Book 14)
Blood Into Wine (Book 15)
Jack In The Box (Book 16)
The Fall Moon (Book 17)
Blood In Babylon (Book 18)
Death In Dexter (Book 19)
Mustang Sally (Book 20)

A Christmas Killing (Book 21)
Mommy's Little Killer (Book 22)
Bleed Out (Book 23)
Dead and Buried (Book 24)
In Hot Blood (Book 25)
Fallen Angels (Book 26)
Knife Edge (Book 27)
Along Came A Spider (Book 28)
Cold Blood (Book 29)
Curtain Call (Book 30)

THE OMEGA SERIES
Dawn of the Hunter (Book 1)
Double Edged Blade (Book 2)
The Storm (Book 3)
The Hand of War (Book 4)
A Harvest of Blood (Book 5)
To Rule in Hell (Book 6)
Kill: One (Book 7)
Powder Burn (Book 8)
Kill: Two (Book 9)
Unleashed (Book 10)
The Omicron Kill (Book 11)
9mm Justice (Book 12)
Kill: Four (Book 13)
Death In Freedom (Book 14)
Endgame (Book 15)

ABOUT US

Right House is an independent publisher created by authors for readers. We specialize in Action, Thriller, Mystery, and Crime novels.

If you enjoyed this novel, then there is a good chance you will like what else we have to offer! Please stay up to date by using any of the links below.

Join our mailing lists to stay up to date -->
righthouse.com/email
Visit our website --> righthouse.com
Contact us --> contact@righthouse.com

 facebook.com/righthousebooks
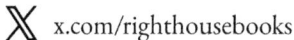 x.com/righthousebooks
instagram.com/righthousebooks

EXCLUSIVE SNEAK PEAK OF...

ALONG CAME A SPIDER

CHAPTER 1

"The crazy thing was—" Detective Justin Campbell clasped his hand over his mouth and half closed his eyes. He had a cigarette between his first and middle fingers, and he sucked on it like it was oxygen and he had severe emphysema. When he had his lungs full, he stretched up his chin and drew the smoke deeper before letting it out in small wafts as he spoke. His voice was like gravel matured in nicotine and whiskey. "Her DNA was at the scene, *on* the victim, fresh. She'd had sex with this guy just before he died." The smoke drifted up into his eyes, and he squinted at me, then at Dehan. "It should have been an open-and-shut case. It *was* an open-and-shut case."

He shrugged. Neither of us said anything. He took a piece of tobacco from his lip and examined it.

"But she wasn't there." He raised his eyes to look at us. "Two hundred people could swear she was more than a hundred and eighty miles away, in Boston. And among them was the Boston police commissioner."

Dehan was leafing through the file while she listened, glancing at him occasionally while he spoke. She was sitting on a faded green sofa in the bay window, with a square of warm morning sunlight on the cushion beside her.

"What makes you so sure it was just before he died? Maybe they hit the sack that morning before he left."

He was already shaking his head before she'd finished, flicking ash into the glass ashtray on the arm of his chair.

"Nah, Frank—you know Frank, the ME." We both nodded that we did. "He examined the body at the scene." He paused to give me a knowing look. "Believe me, that is one examination of a dead body you don't want to watch when you just had dinner! You know what I'm saying?"

I winced, and he went on. "Not only did he have her . . ." He waved the hand with the cigarette around in circles, making small spirals of smoke. "Her *discharge* all over his . . ." He made more spirals. Dehan cut across him.

"He had her vaginal discharge all over his penis?"

He frowned at her. "Yeah, that, but the doc said it was not even dry yet. Like it was *real* recent. Like, they did it and she did him. Badabim badabam! Also"—he turned to me—"and get this, her saliva was all over his chest." He stabbed down with his smoking fingers. "And *in the wound*! How sick is that? I mean, that is . . ." He nodded awhile then shook his head. "That is some special kind of sick."

Dehan found the pictures of the body and handed me one. It showed a naked man in his early forties lying on his back on the floor of his bedroom. There was a lot of blood underneath him, and somewhat less blood on his chest, where there was an ugly wound in the region of his heart. Beyond him was the bed, unmade.

I said, "He was stabbed first in the back; the chest wound was perimortem."

He sucked on his cigarette again, squinting at me through the smoke.

"Yeah, the stab in the back was what killed him. He must've fell down, then she gets on top of him, stabs him in the heart, pulls out the knife, and then the crazy bitch licks his chest."

Dehan was reading a form in the file.

"Prints were on the knife."

Campbell nodded. "Yeah, clear set of prints on the knife."

I made a face that said that didn't impress me much.

"That's to be expected. It was her house."

"Sure, but what is not to be expected is that there were no prints *on top* of hers. Neither were there smudges from a pair of latex gloves. All you've got is his prints and her prints. It's their house, their kitchen, their knife. But nobody else used that knife."

I grunted. "Tell me about Paul Gotlieb. He found the body, right?"

"Paul and Helen Gotlieb live next door, at 2253. Bob, the victim, and Sheila, his wife, lived at 2251. Now, 2251 sits alone in its own grounds, with seven steps going up to the front door. It's a very noticeable house. Now, Paul and Helen live next door, but next door is like thirty or forty feet away. Like I said, the houses aren't connected. So you're not going to hear anything through the walls is what I'm saying. But they're pals, always in and out of each other's houses. Helen and Sheila are best friends, Bob and Paul are best pals. Bob worked from home..."

Dehan interrupted. "He had his own web design company, right?"

"Yeah, IT services kinda thing, successful, he was making money. Paul was an architect and worked from home three days a week, so they saw a lot of each other. So on the night of the murder, Monday, October 1, 2018, at about seven thirty p.m., Paul is taking out the trash, and from his porch he sees Sheila leave the house in a hurry. She runs down the steps to her car and drives away. He's surprised because he thought she had some kind of event in Boston that night. As it turned out he was right, that's where she was, but he swears he recognized her and the car." He shrugged. "They're close friends, right? They see each other most every day. He knows her."

"Did he talk to her?"

"He says he called out to her. Something like, 'Hey, Sheila, how's it going? Aren't you supposed to be in Boston?' Something like that. But she doesn't respond. She gets in the car and drives away. Now he notices the front door is open. He thinks she left in a hurry and forgot to close it, or it didn't close properly, whatever. He dumps the trash and walks over to Bob and Sheila's house. Like I said, the house is in its own grounds, so we're talking about maybe fifty-five or sixty feet from Paul's front door to Bob's front door. He climbs the seven steps, pushes open the door, and calls for Bob. Nothing. But all the lights are on. He calls again a couple of times. Looks in the living room, the kitchen; no sign of Bob anywhere. Now he's beginning to get worried. So he goes upstairs. He's still calling his name. He sees the bedroom door open, and when he steps in, this is what he finds. He freaks, runs downstairs, and calls 911."

He paused to take a final drag on his cigarette before crushing it out in the ashtray while smoke trailed from his nose. Dehan still had the crime scene photographs in her hands, but she was staring at the cold fireplace. I broke the silence.

"So what did you find when you got there?"

"There's Paul Gotlieb sitting on the stoop with his wife, Helen. They've both been crying. He tells me he hasn't touched anything, so we go inside. Upstairs it's just like you see in the pictures. He's naked. Somebody has stabbed him in the back. They've pulled out the knife. He's gone down bleeding profusely. They've got on top of him and stabbed him again in the heart. They pulled out the knife again and dropped it beside the body."

Dehan spoke as though to the fireplace. "He's naked; suggests either the killer surprised him, or he was intimate with the killer."

"Right? That's what I am thinking. Either the killer has crept in and stabbed him in the back without being seen, or she has put her arms around him like she is going to hug him and kiss him, and stabbed him in the embrace. And that kind of fits in some sick way with the saliva on his chest." He looked slightly sick. "Kind of kinky mix of murder and sex. Like she got a kick out of it or something."

Dehan scratched her head and left a couple of long black

strands slightly raised, reflecting the sunlight through the window. A fly buzzed against the glass.

"I thought I read somewhere that Bob and Sheila were splitting up . . . ?"

She gave it the intonation of a question. Campbell gave a dry bark that was meant to be a laugh.

"Right. That was where it started to get complicated. Bob's den is next door to the bedroom. So while the crime scene boys are taking prints and photographs, and Frank is examining the body, I take a stroll into the den." He turned to me and leaned forward slightly. "What do I find there? I find his computer switched on. I find Skype open. I have a look, and I find this is not unusual. He has been using Skype all day. In fact, when Joe and the crime scene boys look at the computer, they find he uses it all day every day for work. And it just so happens he's been on Skype that evening at seven-something. I have a look at the last person he's spoken to." He wagged his finger at me once. "One Sorka Williams. She's a writer, IT geek. She doesn't write books, she writes content for websites. So they work together, a lot. But that is not all they do together a lot. On his desk there are some travel brochures, and he has sent her pictures of those brochures. I'm thinking maybe it's for a website, but it's not. When Joe and the boys had a look at his phone, it became clear they were having an affair—a very serious affair. She's a real looker, twenty-four, real cute, and judging by the messages they were real crazy about each other."

I sighed, trying to visualize the scene. "So, he was alive and talking to Sorka Williams on Skype at seven, and at seven thirty Paul claims he saw Bob's wife—"

Dehan said absently, "Sheila Walklet."

"—Sheila Walklet, leave the house. He entered, found the body, and made the 911 call at seven forty p.m. So that gives us a pretty tight window of forty minutes for Bob to finish his Skype call, go into his bedroom, and get killed."

Dehan looked at me and curled her lip. "Makes you wonder how close Paul and Sheila were."

Campbell nodded. "Right, that was my first thought. Simple, he sees Sheila leave, tells his wife he's taking out the trash, goes over to Bob's house, lets himself in. Upstairs he finds Bob naked in his bedroom, kills him, calls 911. But..."

I was shaking my head. "It raises more questions than it answers. For a start, if Sheila didn't leave the door open, how did he get in?"

Dehan said, "Not impossible or even difficult for him to get a key. Or maybe that part of the story was true, and Sheila did leave the door open."

Aside from a grunt, I ignored her. "Second, if he has a thing for Sheila and jealousy is his motive, why does he then cast suspicion on her? Last, but by no means least, it does not square the circle of Sheila's DNA being on Bob's body while she is giving a talk in Boston."

Dehan held up both hands. "Waitwaitwait! Let's take this one step at a time. Let's say, just for the sake of the argument, that Paul has harbored a secret love for Sheila for a long time. For some reason his feelings have recently come to a head. On the night in question, he either sees Sheila leave or doesn't—it makes no difference for the purposes of my theory—he is going to take out the trash and sees Bob's door open."

I interrupted, "Or he has a key. Those kinds of neighbors often have keys to each other's houses."

"Right. Either way he is suddenly seized by a crazy idea. He takes a knife and some rubber gloves from the kitchen. He dumps the trash, goes into Bob's, puts on the gloves, and kills Bob. He then takes a knife from Bob's kitchen, smears it with blood, and drops it beside the body. He goes downstairs, calls 911, goes home, and on the way dumps the gloves in the garbage, washes the knife, puts it away, and tells his wife Bob has been murdered."

Campbell had been listening with a frown on his face. "But what about..."

"Wait. I'm coming to that. Paul *had* seen Sheila leave—but *earlier* than he said, at maybe two, three, or four o'clock. That's what put the idea into his head to say he'd seen her. But it wasn't right then, it was several hours before."

I said, "She was supposed to have left for Boston late morning."

"But she didn't. Sometimes couples that are breaking up get all nostalgic and amorous. So they hit the sack. After she'd gone, he was too lazy or too busy or both and didn't shower. The rate at which bodily fluids dry is notoriously unreliable. Sure, it was recent, but hours, not minutes. It takes three and a half hours to drive to Boston, more or less. If the conference was at seven, she could have left as late as three or four p.m. If she took an air taxi, she could have left even later."

I made a question with my face and showed it to Campbell. He shrugged.

"It's not impossible, I guess. Sheila did have witnesses that placed her in Boston at midday: waiters, a concierge. But . . ."

Dehan echoed his shrug. "If their marriage was on the rocks, she might have panicked and decided it was smart to get a few witnesses to say she was in Boston all day. That's not so hard to do." She frowned and leafed through the file again. "She'd been a cop, right?"

He nodded. "She was a cop for a few years, then got a job as an insurance investigator, then became a security consultant for insurance companies. Smart lady."

"So if she was a cop, she'd know that the spouse is the first person the cops look at as a possible suspect. We'll have to look good and hard at her alibi." She glanced at him. "No offense."

Campbell smiled. "None taken. Be my guest, Detective Dehan, but we've already done that. You do it again. Maybe you'll find something we missed."

"There's just one other thing I wanted to ask you about." I gave my head a scratch. "Sheila Walklet had been having an affair, right?"

"Yeah. When she discovered Bob and Sorka had been hitting the hay, she got real mad and started having an affair of her own with a guy at her office. Man by the name of Jesus Pinaglia, Mexican. Looks like he has a record back in Mexico, but it got lost or some shit. You know how it goes. My own feeling was that he was a creep, and I thought for a while maybe they were accomplices, but he had an alibi and, worse still, there was zero evidence to implicate him." He sighed. "And even if they was working together, it still didn't explain how she could be in two places at the same time!"

"She had motive," said Dehan, reading a form in the file, "and then some. Not only was her husband cheating on her, she got a handsome payout from his life insurance."

"Yeah," Campbell rumbled, nodding. "Don't forget the prenup too. If they divorced, she was not entitled to a damn penny of his company. And the worst part of it is, she increased his insurance just one month before, right around the time she found out he was cheating on her. She never disclosed the amount. She didn't have to, because she had an airtight alibi." He waved his finger in the air. "But there is no question in my mind, none at all, that she killed her husband. But how? That's the question. At the time of his death, she was almost two hundred miles away, in Boston. But everything, all the forensic evidence, says she was here, screwing her husband—excuse me, Detective Dehan—and in more ways than one."

"Be my guest."

"Screwing her husband and sticking a knife in his back. With motive. The two oldest motives known to man." He shrugged again. "I know you two got a reputation for cracking these cold cases, but I'm telling you, whatever about your theory of an air taxi, you got your work cut out for you on this one."

He pulled a cigarette from his packet, tapped the end on his lighter, and poked it in his mouth. Then he sighed and stared at his Zippo for a moment before shaking his head and lighting up.

CHAPTER 2

Some time later we stepped out of Detective Justin Campbell's house and into the breezy, briny sunshine of Clarence Avenue, on Eastchester Bay. I paused for a moment to look at the stars and stripes flapping over his door, then followed Dehan down the path, through his front yard, and out to my ancient burgundy Jaguar parked by the gate. She sat against the hood and crossed her arms.

"What's the time?" she said. "I could use a coffee."

I glanced at my watch. "Eleven. Yeah, let's grab a coffee, then decide how we tackle this."

We took a stroll to the fisherman's wharf on the corner, where we sat out back, drinking coffee and eating muffins under a blue parasol, watching the boats dart and heel on the water.

Dehan waved a muffin at me. "The investigation failed because Campbell got hung up on trying to understand how the impossible happened."

I watched a sail like a pale wraith lean over and skip across the small waves. I made a face like maybe she was right and broke my muffin in two. She went on.

"It's like he was fed the data, her DNA says she was in New York having sex with her husband at the same time as she was giving a talk in Boston, and he went, 'Cannot compute, cannot compute, cannot compute.'"

I gave a small laugh. "So?"

"So obviously that is impossible, so we eliminate it. It is established that she was at the house with Bob and they had sex. It is also established conclusively that she was in Boston from roughly six o'clock onward—waiters and concierge notwithstanding. Now, note, Stone, the *time* is established in only one of those two cases. Therefore"—she waved the muffin at me again and broke it in half—"as a person *cannot be* in two places at the same time, we have no choice but to conclude that she was in New York having sexual congress with her husband *before* she went to Boston. *Quod erat demonstrandum.*"

"My baby is growing up. You have moved on from Mickey Spillane to Sherlock Holmes."

"Yeah, I am trying to broaden my vocabulary. Point is, Stone, she *was* in both places, as all the evidence demonstrates, but it had to be at different times. We know when she was in Boston, so she had to be in New York before that."

A small puff of cloud passed momentarily across the face of the sun, casting a shadow over the darting sails in the harbor.

"There is an irresistible logic to that argument, Dehan."

"Thank you. Now, we know it takes just over three hours by car. So if she went by car, she had to leave at three o'clock or three thirty the latest. If she left after three thirty, the only way she could do it was by taking an air taxi. We would have to look into that, but I figure she'd need two hours minimum. So if she killed him, that puts the time of death between three and four thirty."

"Good; again, irresistible logic."

She had bitten into the muffin and now sat ruminating like a sheep, staring first at the dark water and then at me. "The problem is," she said, "that we know Bob was killed after seven o'clock because at seven o'clock he was talking to Sorka Williams."

"Apparently."

"What do you mean, 'apparently'?"

I shook my head. "Nothing special, except that we will have to confirm that ourselves by talking to her in person. We can't take anything for granted."

She chewed slowly, staring at me, then swallowed.

"It might have been audio? Might have been texts that were deleted after?"

"We don't know. The report just says that they spoke via Skype. I want to hear the details from Sorka."

"Fair enough. Is that where you want to start?"

"Maybe. But keep going, Dehan. You were saying that we know that at seven he was talking to Sorka, so Sheila could not have killed him earlier that afternoon."

She nodded. "And unless she surprises us with some aspect of their Skype conversation that was not included in the original report, that is what it is going to prove. So we are left with an inevitable conclusion. And that is, that Sheila Walklet did not kill her husband. And that means that somebody else did."

I thought about it, and after a while I nodded. "It does seem to follow irresistibly."

"But?"

"But there is the question of the saliva in the wound."

She shrugged. "It could have been pulled in by the knife."

"I guess, but I can't see Frank making that kind of mistake. We need to talk to him about that."

"Eliminate the impossible, Stone. Isn't that Holmes' dictum? Whatever you're left with, however unlikely, is the truth."

"I know. So what are we left with if we eliminate Sheila?" I held up my thumb. "Your theory about Paul, which does *not* carry an irresistible logic. It is based purely on the fact that he was alone in the house at approximately the time Bob died."

"He had opportunity. He may be the only person who had."

I grunted and held up my index. "Two, Jesus Pinaglia, Sheila's lover, who at least has something like a conceivable motive, but as Campbell told us, they could find no evidence at all to suggest that he killed Bob, plus he had an alibi."

She made a derisory noise, blowing air through her lips. "Some alibi! It's in the file. You should read the files sometimes, Stone. They're full of, you know, relevant information."

"That's what I have you for, Dehan, to read the files for me. I know what his alibi was. He was with a woman who glories in the name of Cherry Candy. A lady of the night with many assets but little virtue, at least of the moral variety."

"Meaning he could have, and probably did, buy that alibi."

"Still, Dehan, all that gets us is that he *could* have done it. It does not show that he did."

"So we need to trace Cherry Candy and talk to her." She pulled out her cell, scrolled through her address book, and made a call.

"Yeah, Dominguez, it's Dehan." She made a face that could wilt lettuce. "Yeah, shut up. Listen, you still in Vice . . . ? That's funny. I never heard that one before . . . You done? I know, a lot of people tell me that when I invite them to give me their opinion on my character. So I need you to find an escort who goes by the name of Cherry Candy. She was around in 2018, 2019. I need to know where she is now." She listened a moment. "Yeah, appreciate it. Thanks."

She hung up. I said, "Your trouble is you're too nice."

"You could be right. He's going to ask around and get back to me." She thrust out her bottom lip and spread her hands. "He—Pinaglia—figures he has a good thing going with Sheila and maybe they have a future together. Bob is doing well, but if Sheila divorces him, the prenup means she gets nothing. He figures if he kills Bob before they are divorced, she might get the company and all his money."

"Feasible."

"Damn right it is."

"Okay." I drained my coffee. "Let's go talk to Sorka."

She picked up a crumb of muffin from her plate and flicked it at me with deadly aim.

"You still think Sheila did it, don't you? You are not thinking logically, Stone."

"I don't think, Little Grasshopper, I *be*!"

It was a fifteen-minute drive to Sorka's house on Olmstead Avenue, overlooking Pugsley Creek. It was a modern, two-story house in redbrick and white clapboard, with a garage and a small triangular garden in the front yard.

Dehan paused to look the place over while I walked down the path and rang on the bell. I heard feet clattering down the stairs, and a moment later the door opened.

The first thing you noticed about Sorka Williams was that she smiled a lot. She was Caribbean, about twenty-eight, with lots of wild hair, big brown eyes that seemed to shine with their own light, a pretty, smiling face, and the kind of body it was hard not to look at.

She looked at me a moment, then glanced at Dehan behind me.

"Yes?"

I showed her my badge. "Detectives John Stone and Carmen Dehan, New York Police Department. We were wondering if we could talk to you for a few minutes about Bob Walklet."

The smile faded from her face and was replaced by an expression that was hard to fathom. There was surprise, sadness, maybe even desolation.

"Oh." She glanced unconsciously at her living room. "Sure, come on in. Has something happened?"

"No." I smiled and shook my head. We stepped inside, and she closed the door behind us. "We run a cold-case unit at the Forty-Third, and we've just picked up the case."

She led us into a bright, minimalist living room with a cream IKEA sofa and armchairs, a giant TV on a stand, and sliding glass doors onto a big backyard. She sat on the sofa, and Dehan and I each took a chair. She looked at Dehan a moment.

"I'm not sure I can tell you anything I didn't already tell the other detective."

"Don't worry about it. We just like to get it from the horse's mouth. Sometimes the smallest detail, that only you can know, can open up a whole new line of inquiry."

She nodded. "Okay." She pressed her palms together and thrust them between her knees. "What do you want to know?"

I answered, "Tell us about your relationship with Bob. How did that come about?"

She smiled and sighed. Her eyes went down to her hands.

"I'm a writer. I'm an expert in IT, but at heart I am a writer. I love words." She glanced at me, like she expected me to laugh. "I'm not a novelist or anything like that—yet. But I am working on it. Most people, when you tell them you're a writer, they try to put you down, patronize you, ridicule you . . ." She trailed off and shrugged with her hands still clasped between her knees. "But Bob was different. He was kind, and very supportive."

"How did you meet?"

"He had a lot of friends on Facebook, and he posted that he was looking for a talented young writer to create content for websites. It turned out we had a mutual friend and—" She released her left hand and jerked her thumb north. "I used to have an apartment on Lafayette, like, literally ten or fifteen minutes' walk from him. So Maggie, that was the mutual friend, messaged me and said, like, this guy is looking for a writer and he will pay you to write!" Her face lit up, and she laughed. "That just doesn't happen, you know! So I got in touch and, I mean, he was like twenty years older than me, but straight away it was like, wow!"

Dehan smiled. "You were attracted to each other."

"And some. But he was married, and nothing happened for a long time. There are things you just don't do, right? But I used to go over there to work a lot, and we would like talk, and I would write. We had great rapport, and we did a *lot* of work that way. We were a very productive team. Then . . ."

She paused, glanced at Dehan, and turned to me. "I feel so ashamed, but"—she gave a small laugh that was oddly reluctant—"we began to talk a lot more. He was just such a good, kind person. He was *human*. You know what I mean?" The question was directed at Dehan, who nodded. "Human and humane. I just fell completely in love with him. He was a dream come true. We talked a lot about my work—my real work—about his dreams for the future, the things he wanted to achieve. I never dared to believe that maybe he felt the same way about me, but I couldn't help noticing that more and more often, when he talked about his hopes and dreams for the future, there was less and less mention of Sheila." She laughed again. "And he would always find a way to sneak me in somehow. I'd have the house next door, or he'd build me an office next to his."

She frowned and looked at the floor. Her hands found their way between her knees again.

"I felt so conflicted. They were married. They were a family. She obviously loved him, and when I had arrived on the scene, he still loved her. I hated the idea of breaking them up, that I had come between them, but at the same time, the *thrill* I felt—" She shook her head. "The thought that he might be falling in love with me was just so wonderful. I didn't know what to do. Then one day, I arrived for work, Sheila was out, she usually was, and he was very serious. He told me to sit down because he wanted to talk to me about something very important." She gave a small laugh. "I thought he was going to fire me, but he told me—" She shrugged, and her face lit up with bemused joy. "He was in love with me, that he was going to leave his wife, and he wanted us to make a life and a family together."

Dehan said, "That must have been a shock."

"Shock?" She gave a high-pitched giggle that made me laugh. "It blew me away. I was a wreck, a joyful wreck. I couldn't think. I didn't know what to do or what to say. He told me he didn't want to have any kind of sexual relationship with me until he had told his wife they were finished, and after that only if I felt the same way as him. He didn't want an affair, and he didn't want a short-term relationship. He was in love, and he wanted us to live together, or be married, whatever I wanted. He was so cute and old-fashioned. You can imagine I was kind of out of my mind. So he told me to go and think about it for a day or two, and let him know."

"That's pretty intense."

"Yeah, it was pretty intense. So I left, and I called him when I was halfway home. I told him yes, I loved him and adored him and I wanted to spend the rest of my life with him. I ran all the way back, and we spent the rest of the afternoon talking about the future."

I asked, "And did he tell Sheila?"

"Yeah, that was a Friday, I think, and that weekend they talked."

"When was that?"

"I am not great with dates, but it was summer. I guess it would have been like July or August, 2018."

Dehan winced. "That must have made things pretty awkward."

"Not so much as you might think. Her lawyer advised her not to move out until the terms of the divorce were settled. But she was hardly ever there before, she was always going away because of work, and after he'd told her about us, I think she went and looked for a lover just to get back at him. So we were able to spend a lot of time together, and make plans." A look of infinite sadness touched her face. "So many plans, so many dreams. All gone now."

"He told her he was going to divorce her?"

"Oh yes. Like I said, she wasn't going to move out until the terms of the divorce were settled. They had both signed a prenuptial agreement, but she was going to contest it. There was a lot of wrangling and negotiating. They were two very tough months. But we didn't fall apart. We supported each other, and we were doing good." She paused again, hesitated. "The problem was his business. It was becoming very successful, and he was making a lot of money. He was on his way to becoming"—she grinned at Dehan and nodded—"actually rich! Like, *really* rich. But if her lawyers managed to break the prenup, then he was scared she could take half the business. So we had to be very careful and try to reach a settlement where he didn't risk losing everything he had worked for."

I said, "So, let me get this one fact straight in my mind. He had asked her for a divorce."

"Yes, and the lawyers were already negotiating. Basically, the deal they were looking for was, what was he prepared to give her in exchange for her not challenging the legality of the prenuptial agreement."

"And had they come to some kind of agreement?"

"Not really. She was playing hardball. I don't think she was that interested in reaching an agreement. I think all she really wanted was to destroy him. And us."

CHAPTER 3

She had risen and was standing silhouetted against the glass doors, staring out at the backyard with her back to us. She had been crying and was now noisily, unselfconsciously, blowing her nose.

"I'm sorry, this has been a bit of a shock. Not a day goes by that I don't think about him, how life could have been. But I guess I had just accepted that the cops had given up."

She turned to face us. Her eyes and her nose were swollen, but it didn't detract from her looks.

"What we did was wrong." Her face went into a kind of spasm, somewhere between weeping and laughing. "But we were like kids. We were crazy about each other, and that makes you . . ." She sighed, smiling. "Well, I guess you're just so happy all the time it's hard to think straight. I never wanted to hurt Sheila. I had nothing against her. She was nice. And Bob tried to do things right. He was honest with her and told her just as soon as he and I had talked." Her gaze dropped, and she looked down at her hands. "But I guess it must have hurt her a lot."

"Sorka." She glanced at me. "Can you tell us about the last conversation you had with Bob?"

She nodded, looked down at her hands again. "I'll never

forget it as long as I live. I hadn't been to his house for a couple of days. The situation between them was pretty tense, and we were trying to avoid escalating it. So we had our computers networked and we'd been working mainly via Skype, email, that kind of thing. He'd been to my apartment a few times too." She stopped, took a deep breath. "At about six thirty? Maybe a quarter to seven, I don't remember the exact time, he called me."

She smiled down at her palms, like she was holding the memory there. For a moment her expression was radiant, but then her bottom lip curled in, and the tears spilled from her eyes.

"He was so happy. He said he had reached an agreement with Sheila. Her lawyer had accepted that the prenup could not be broken, and they were going to drop their attempt to challenge it, if he would agree to some minor concessions."

Dehan asked, "What concessions?"

Sorka took a deep, damp breath. "Gosh, to sell the house, and she would take sixty percent instead of fifty, the car, a couple of paintings that were worth something. Things like that. He said it was all worth it and cheap at the price to get her off his back and out of our lives. We talked briefly about work, but what he was really excited about was that he was going to book a holiday for us. We were going to go away to Barbados for a week. He was so happy, so excited. He was really like a big kid. Then he said he had to go. Those . . ." She bit her lip, and the tears welled again. "Those were the last words he ever said to me. 'I have to go.'"

"Did he say why?"

She blew her nose and returned to the sofa.

"That was a problem when the first detective came to talk to me."

I frowned. "A problem why?"

"Because I wanted to be really careful not to let my own feelings prejudice me, or warp my memory. And I couldn't help feeling that Detective"—she closed her eyes a moment—"Campbell, Detective Campbell, was almost egging me on to say that Sheila had arrived. And the honest truth is, I am not sure. It is *possible* that Bob said she had arrived and he had to go. But it is equally possible he just said, 'I have to go,' and I assumed she had arrived. The *feeling* was that somebody had come into the house, and the only person who had a key was her."

We were quiet, then she added, "And that felt so wrong." She gave a small laugh and glanced at Dehan as though for support. "I told Bob we should have just moved in together. Screw the house, screw the divorce. But he said if he moved out, it would weaken his legal position. I didn't give a damn about the legal position. I just wanted them to get divorced and for us to start our own life." For a moment all the joy seemed to drain out of her face. "Looks like I was right. We were the couple, not them. We were making plans for the future, talking about buying our own house, having children—hell, we even took out insurance on each other..."

Dehan interrupted. "You took out life insurance?"

"Bob arranged it. He was all about that kind of thing. When we started talking about buying a house, going on holiday together, that kind of stuff, he said we needed insurance. I told him then, all I wanted was him. If he'd listened to me, instead of worrying about mortgages and insurance and negotiating positions, he'd still be alive now."

I asked, "What makes you say that, Sorka?"

She shrugged. "He wouldn't have been in that house, alone, would he? He would have been with me."

I nodded. "Sorka, aside from Sheila's obvious motive, can you think of anybody else who might have wanted to hurt Bob?"

She sighed, turning her handkerchief over in her fingers.

"They told me Sheila was in Boston at the time he died, and could not have done it. After the way she treated Bob when she found out he wanted a divorce, I had plenty of reason to resent Sheila." She shook her head. "But I can't honestly put my hand on my heart and say I believe she killed him. Maybe I'm naïve, but I don't see her as a killer. She was bitter, angry, hurt, but all of that was understandable.

"If you're asking me who I think did it, then I would have to say her boyfriend. I'm not great with names, but he was a Mexican guy, Jesus . . ."

Dehan said, "Pinaglia?"

"Yeah. He showed up at the house with her once, after things had gone south in a big way. She wanted to flaunt him. He was horrible, with a pencil moustache and a shiny, double-breasted suit. And cruel eyes. Cruel, cruel eyes."

"His motive?"

"Simple. If Bob died before the divorce, she got everything, and he got it with her. But under the terms of the prenup, she got half of the joint property and none of the business. I know he had an alibi for the night of the murder, but men like him can arrange alibis. I am pretty sure he killed Bob. I think maybe Sheila knew about it and turned a blind eye. I am not sure about that. But I am sure he killed Bob."

I gave my head a one-fingered scratch.

"So what happened to the business?"

"Bob's Web?" Her smile was ironic, with a twist of bitterness that looked out of place on her face. "Another tragic waste. He was a real artist. I don't know how to explain this, but he was a nice guy, a genuine, real nice guy. He was generous, good, kind, and all of that came across in his work. You saw one of his websites and it made you smile. Your customers saw one of his websites and they just wanted to be part of it and buy your product. That was him all over. He engaged you, pulled you in, made you feel a part of things. When he died, the company died with him."

"I'm sorry." I looked at Dehan. "You have anything else?"

She shook her head, and we stood.

Sorka followed us to the door, and as we stepped out into the sunshine, she frowned at me.

"Do you think you might make more progress this time?"

"That's impossible to say, Sorka. We'll do our best, and we'll keep you posted."

She nodded and glanced at Dehan. "Anything you need, just ask."

We climbed in the old Jag, and as Dehan slammed the door she said, "How come Campbell gave up so easy on Pinaglia?"

"He didn't."

I turned the key in the ignition, and the big old engine growled.

"He didn't?"

I pulled away and started back up Olmstead Avenue.

"No. Pinaglia had an alibi, and Campbell didn't think he could shake it. That to you is giving up easy. Campbell is a collie, perhaps a German shepherd; you are a rottweiler. To you, giving up at all is giving up easy."

She turned away and looked out of the window, trying not to smile.

"Yeah, well, it looks to me like Pinaglia and Sheila are our best suspects, and Pinaglia's alibi is pretty weak. *That* to me is giving up easy. We need to find Cherry Candy and give her a good shake, see what drops out of her foliage."

"Yup, but first I want to see exactly what priors he has. It all seems a bit vague to me. I am not sure exactly who we are dealing with. Is he a petty thief who swam across the border to start a new life, or are we talking Sinaloa hit man with a whitewashed past?"

"Shouldn't that be whom?"

"What?"

"Whom. I am not sure *whom* we are dealing with."

"Yes, Dehan, it should."

"Thank you. Didn't you have a pal at the bureau?"

"Bernie."

"Pull that string. If you go through official channels, we'll be chasing Pinaglia in Zimmer frames by the time they get back to you."

I took out my phone, set it in the cradle, and dialed Bernie.

"I don't believe it. Blast from the past! I won't ask you how you're doing, I'll cut to the chase and ask you what you want!" He laughed. "You still owe me three thousand six hundred and fifty-five beers from all the times I pulled your nuts out of the fire!"

"Make it three thousand six hundred and fifty-six. How you doing, Bernie?"

"Great, what do you want? We can catch up when you finally invite me to dinner."

"Jesus Pinaglia, Mexican, resident in New York, maybe involved with Sheila Walklet, onetime cop, now security consultant to various insurance companies."

"What about him?"

"Word is he has previous in Mexico, but for some reason it's not easy to get hold of those previous. Can you get them? I have a feeling usual channels might be clogged."

"I'll have a look, see if we have a file on him. I have a few pals at the DEA who might know something."

"I appreciate it."

"Yeah, yeah. One of these days I am going to turn up on your doorstep with a suitcase and move in with you, just to give you time to catch up on everything you owe me. Is Carmen there with you?"

"Uh-huh."

"Carmen, what the hell are you doing with this loser? Call me, we'll do lunch, and I'll set you straight about him."

"You have a deal."

We promised to meet soon and hung up.

We stopped at the deli to get beef sandwiches and coffee and arrived at our desks at one thirty. I spent the next hour going through the phone records and financials of the deceased and managed to discover exactly nothing except what I already knew: that Bob was crazy about Sorka and Sorka was crazy about Bob. He had indeed been about to book a holiday for them in Barbados, and his company had been surprisingly successful.

What did come as a small surprise was that a lot of the exchanges between Sheila and Bob were not as acrimonious as I had come to expect. I looked across the desk at Dehan, who was staring fixedly at the screen of her laptop with a paper cup of cold coffee halfway to her mouth.

"Some of these text messages between Sheila and Bob—"

"When?" she said, without looking at me.

"When? About a week before he died, roughly."

"Uh-huh," she said to the screen, "what about them?"

"Some of them are quite friendly, as though they like each other."

Now she frowned at me. "Yeah? All of them or just some of them?"

"No." I shook my head. "Some of them, but more than I would have expected. She seems genuinely upset that he is leaving her. Other times she is positively venomous."

"Never trust a jilted woman." She pointed at the papers in my hand. "She is luring him in. She wants to make him be unfaithful to his new love. Looks like she managed it too. According to the DNA."

I looked back at one of the last messages and read aloud, "When this is all over, Bob, do you think we will ever manage to be friends?"

"Ha!" I looked up, a little startled. "See?" she said. "You guys are so helplessly naïve. You read that and you think, 'Ah, she wants to be friends.' I hear that and I think, 'The bitch is closing in for the kill!'"

"Seriously?"

"Seriously. What did he answer, 'I sure hope so. You will always be very special to me'?"

I laughed. "Almost verbatim. 'I hope so, Sheila. I am sorry about the way things turned out, but you will always be very special to me.'"

"See? And what did Miss Special do? A couple of days later she seduces him and leaves for her conference in Boston, while Pinaglia moves in and kills Bob, leaving her DNA all over his body, knowing, like the cop she is, that the crime scene boys will find it and report it and Sorka will live the rest of her life with the knowledge that the last woman to have sex with the love of her life was Sheila, not her. Very special and want to be friends, my ass!"

"Remind me never to divorce you."

"That's okay," she said, looking back at the screen. "We would always be friends . . ."

"I sure hope so," I said without smiling. "You will always be very special to me."

"I have something here. January 2019, *Brooklyn Heights Gazette*: 'The case against Mr. Jesus Pinaglia, in which it was alleged he had beaten his partner so badly she was admitted to intensive care, collapsed yesterday after his partner, Sheila Walklet, withdrew her complaint against him, alleging she had slipped and fallen down the stairs.'"

I grunted. "Where is your bitch closing in for the kill now? Call the Eighty-Fourth, see if they have an address for these two. Yeah?"

This last was said into the telephone, which had started to ring.

"John, Bernie, how's it hangin'? Listen, I spoke to some people here at the bureau and at the DEA. Your man is basically a small-time hood. To say he was connected to the Sinaloa Cartel would be to overstate things. He's from Hermosillo, so he was in the Sinaloa area, and he did jobs for families who were connected to families who were connected to Sinaloa. The son of a bitch was lucky, so nothing ever stuck, but it seems he was an enforcer, and he may have either done a couple of hits or gone along for the ride. Either way, 2015 he left Mexico and moved to L.A., then east to New York. Same story, mixes with bad company, is always there when shit goes down, but he is the original Mr. Teflon. Nothing sticks."

"Not even shit."

"Not even that. You ain't going to get any official records from the cops in Hermosillo either. He obviously did somebody a favor somewhere along the line, and whatever record he had was wiped when he moved north of the border."

"Thanks, Bernie, I owe you."

"Yeah? We're coming over, me and the wife, at the weekend. I expect caviar, champagne..."

"We'll do it. Thanks, Bernie."

I hung up and looked at Dehan. She said, "Hicks Street, 163, Brooklyn Heights."

Scan the QR code below to purchase ALONG CAME A SPIDER.
Or go to: righthouse.com/along-came-a-spider

Printed in Dunstable, United Kingdom

64919034R00129